THE
Enemy
TRAP

MAREN MOORE

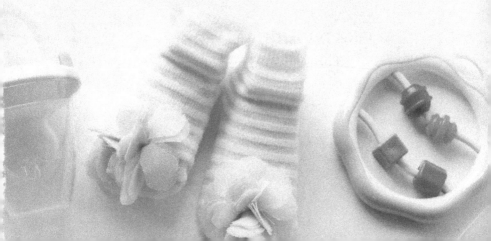

Cover Design: Cat with TRC Designs

Formatting: Maren Moore

About The Book

The Enemy Trap, is a hockey romance with a twist. Throw in a fake fiancé, a surprise baby, and the banter of enemies turned lovers and you have a recipe for disaster. Right?

If you enjoy this over the top man, and his woman, please leave a review on Amazon. It would mean so much to me!

* * *

Blurb

Hayes Davis is America's sweetheart, the #1 hockey player in the country, and my fake fiancé.
Simple, right? It would be, if my betrothed were anyone else.

But it turns out America's sweetheart is arrogant, selfish, and a guy I have no intentions of letting break my heart again.

It was never supposed to happen.
But then one night changes everything.

Now, he's not only my pretend fiancé but my very real baby daddy.

How can two people who hate each other pull off the lie of a lifetime while figuring out how to raise a child together?

Everything between us was supposed to be fake, but I'm not pretending anymore.

To my real life Holly
I can't imagine my life without you by my side.
I love you.

This one is for you.

MAREN MOORE

Playlist

Name(feat. Tori Kelly) - Justin Bieber

Hell You Raised- Mae Estes

Drunk (And I don't Wanna go Home)- Elle King & Miranda Lambert

Somebody Like That- Tenille Arts

Easily- Bruno Major

Can't Help Falling In Love- Haley Reinhart

How You Get The Girl- Taylor Swift

Bad Liar- Selena Gomez

High Horse- Kacey Musgraves

Why Haven't I met You?- Cameron Dallas

Wild(feat. Gary Clark Jr.)- John Legend

Thief- Ansel Elgort

Me Without You- Ashe

Till Forever Falls Apart- Ashe, FINNEAS

Click to listen to the full playlist on Spotify

CHAPTER ONE
Sophia

It seems fitting that I'm ringing in the dreaded big "three-oh" wine drunk on my couch in granny panties and a semi fashionable muumuu. Honestly, if that isn't a birds-eye view of my life, then I don't know what is.

I'm not just a little drunk—I'm a lotta drunk. Like, call your ex and cry on the phone, professing your love for him—even though he cheated on you with your cousin—kind of drunk. Trust me, I hope I forget it by the time morning rolls around.

Highly, highly unlikely.

"Soph, are you listening?" my best friend Holly asks. She's sitting on the arm of my hot pink loveseat, engrossed in the sub-par job she's doing of painting her toes candy apple red.

"Umm, no. Sorry, I was reliving the word vomit that just spewed from my mouth," I groan, dropping my head into my hands. This is not how I envisioned the whole "death to my twenties" party. But that's what happens when you're the last of your single friends. Everyone's married and has kids, and I'll forever be stuck being the cool aunt.

"Tell me again why I thought it would be a good idea to call him? This is going to suck a lot more when I'm hungover and semi clear-headed."

Holly shrugs. "I have no clue why you do half the shit you do, Soph. But...I said, Scott and I made a sex schedule. You know, with Brady teething and Gracie in dance, we really wanted to nail down a time." She grins, "Get it, nail? No, but seriously, how boring and predictable is my life that we have to *schedule* sex. I've officially reached my peak. It's only downhill from here."

"At least you have someone to have sex with and who *wants* to have sex with you."

She finally looks up from her toes and rolls her eyes, "Yes, sixty seconds of missionary and a faked orgasm is honestly something to look forward to."

Okay, she had a point. Still, I'd take a fake orgasm over none at all.

"Ugh, if you'd stop dating guys like Horndog Harry, this wouldn't be a problem." Her tone softens when she sees my expression, a mixture of hurt and regret. "I just hate to see you get hurt over and over by the same type of guy—scared of commitment and couldn't keep his dick in his pants if his life depended on it. Honestly, I don't know what the appeal is with him. You are definitely a ten, and he's like...a three, at best."

"It's not like I purposefully attract assholes, Hol! Apparently, I have a sign on my forehead that says, 'Please fuck me up.' And I'm a solid seven, not a ten."

She rolls her eyes and stands abruptly, setting down the nail polish on my second-hand coffee table and stomping over to where I sit dejectedly on the arm of the couch. At five-eight, she towers over me. Her dark hair is always ten kinds of hot mess, but she pulls it off flawlessly. Holly is the only person I know who could have six days of unwashed hair, dark bags under her eyes, be wearing the same shirt as yesterday, and *still* look like a supermodel straight off the cover of Vogue. It's ridiculously unfair.

"Listen, enough of this sad bullshit! It's your birthday, and we're celebrating, not crying into our beers."

"We're drinking wine...." I squint at her, trying to figure out where she's going with this.

"Whatever. You get it. Oh! Wait," she snaps her fingers. "I've got an idea. I know exactly what you need to cheer you up, and it'll be a stepping stone in the path of getting over HH and under someone else."

Here we go.

I drain my wine in one long gulp that seems to go on forever. My head spins as I swallow down the alcohol, but screw it, I'm in. In like Flynn....

She disappears into my room and comes back moments later holding the box of photos I have stashed under my bed that I wasn't even aware she knew about.

"You hussy, how did you even know about those?"

Holly rolls her eyes. "Because you're a sentimental bitch. But, no longer! We're burning this shit, and you're going to enjoy every single second of it. Goodbye to the little dick, shitty cheater of a fiancé, and hello to a brand new Sophia St. James. You're hot, single, and a solid nine."

She smirks, holding out the box and shaking it back and forth with a shimmy, as if to entice me.

What could it hurt? Maybe it'll help me let go of some of the anger I've been holding in. Lord knows I'm drunk enough to forget it in the morning.

"Fine."

I take the box from her and remove the lid. Maybe she's right; maybe it is time to let go of the past and move forward. Harry doesn't deserve me, and he obviously deserves my slutty, homewrecking whore of a cousin. Those two are a match made in Heaven. If anything, my cousin did me a favor.

"I need something harder for this. Jose, my darling, come to me," I sing-song, dancing over to the fridge.

Don't judge me. I'm going to drown my sorrow in the only man who will never break my heart.

This conversation is making me think too much about my sad, boring life. I'm stuck in the same town I grew up in: same people, same faces, same places.

Broke. Thirty. And single. *Probably forever.*

I have every reason to cry into my beer. Wine. Bottle of tequila. Whatever.

"Alright, I've decided," I tell Holly as she's rifling through my junk drawer for a lighter. "One more night of feeling sorry for myself, and then I'm going to put my big girl panties on, go back to the foundation, ask for my job back, apologize for my momentary lapse in judgment, and grow up. I mean, I'm *thirty*," I whisper, like it's a secret I want no one to hear.

You see, I might have fallen off the deep end a tiny, minuscule amount when I found out I was being cheated on—I quit my job and wallowed on the couch for two weeks straight until Holly came over, fumigated my apartment, and made me shower.

It's not that I hate my job per se, but I feel stuck. Like I'm never going to be anything more than I am right now.

The boring job, the cheating fiancé, the backstabbing friends. Turning thirty is really making me open my eyes and see the bigger picture.

Okay, so it's only been like three hours, but still. I'm a changed woman.

"Got it! Let's go." She thrusts the lighter at me and grabs my hand, pulling me out the backdoor, even though I'm in a muumuu that barely covers my ass. "Wait, I want pictures of this as you *literally* send the old you up in flames. Like a phoenix rising from the fucking ashes, Soph."

Jesus, why did I agree to this? She is entirely too excited about lighting shit on fire.

Together, we light the photos and watch the memories blaze. The fire crackles and pops as it destroys a part of my life I'm not all that sorry to see go. Holly's right...I do feel lighter. Maybe it's the fact that I know this box is no longer going to be stuffed under my bed, waiting for me to pull the photos out and relive the memories over and over again. Or, maybe it's the fact that HH is a douchebag, and deep down I've always known it—I just never wanted to admit it. Catching him with Emily wasn't surprising, at least not now, after the fact. I should've seen the signs.

I should've realized that I was a ten and he was a six, at best.

And that's not just my man Jose talking.

"To stupid assholes who cheat and break our hearts, only to make us stronger." Holly raises the bottle of tequila and takes a sip, her face scrunching in distaste as it burns going down.

"You're married, Hol. Happily, remember?" I laugh, snatching the bottle from her.

"This is about you, not me." Linking her arm in mine, she drags me back towards the house. "Now that you've let go of the past, it's time to move forward. We're setting you up with a dating profile and finding you Mr. Right. We'll think of a good bio that screams, 'Crazy, but not crazy enough to slash your tires.' Guys love crazy bitches. Trust me."

"Uh, no. Absolutely not."

"Really? What happened to the brave, bad ass, solid ten Sophia who just burned every memory of her piece of shit ex? Go take a shower; you've got ashes in your hair. Symbolic, I'm telling ya."

Half a bottle of tequila and a lot of tears later, my still delicate, broken heart lays in tatters on the floor. Add in a shower, more tears, and another signature muumuu, snuggled on the couch with my best friend, and it's a birthday I'll never forget.

The beginning of a new chapter in the messy book of my life.

"Oh, hell," Holly breathes, looking at her phone like it's grown two heads.

"What?"

She flips the phone around, showing me the screen.

I groan.

On the screen is the one person I despise more than HH, and that's saying a lot. Hayes Davis.

Of course, it's another gossip magazine and another scandal. The guy gets himself in more shit than a Kardashian.

"You have got to be kidding me. Does he *want* to destroy his career? Is being a rich, professional hockey player not enough for him? Gross. I mean, not that I keep up with him or anything, but he's on the cover of a different magazine every week with a new scandal in hand."

Holly gives me a knowing smile. "You know, he was voted Hollywood's Most Eligible Bachelor this year."

"Gross. Hope they had a spot for his enormous ego too."

"Yep. He called Scott last week to talk to him about it. Those two gossip on the phone more than we do."

I gag, sticking my finger down my throat for dramatic effect.

"Out of every guy in the world, they chose him. Didn't their mamas teach them that looks are deceiving?"

She rolls her eyes, "You two are ridiculous. Neither of you have moved on since high school."

"Well, that's because...because he's...Hayes Davis! Arrogant. Egotistical. Vain as they come. Ringing a bell? He *is* Scott's best friend, and for whatever reason, your kids' godfather. You should be well aware of how vile he is."

"Well, unfortunately, the world seems to disagree. Introducing Mr. Hollywood's Most Eligible Bachelor." She grins.

Hayes Davis. America's sweetheart and my number one enemy. Yep, even over HH and his cheating pencil dick.

I'd rather use cardboard tampons than spend another second of my time talking about him.

"No, but really, you guys would be so cute together, Soph. Maybe it's time you stop fake hating him and let me and Scott hook you up. He's hot—you can't deny it. Remember, we're leaving the past in the past?"

"Hol! He's your husband's best friend," I cry, my eyes wide.

Shrugging, she looks back at her computer, "So? He is on *People's* Sexiest Men Alive list, so it's merely an observation of fact."

"Too bad they don't account for how big egos are when they choose them, or Hayes would be screwed. I think he's making up for what he lacks in dick size."

"Sophia St. James, you are so hot for him. Stop lying."

Another gag, and I'm five seconds from puking on my Goodwill couch. Hot pink velvet and puke do not mix. I can think of at least ten torture activities I'd prefer over being in the same room with Hayes. Thankfully, even though he's Scott's best friend, he's busy warming every puck bunny's bed from here to Seattle, so I rarely have to be subjected to seeing him.

Only for the kids' birthdays and the occasional holiday, which is more than enough for me. The less the better.

I don't like to give Scott shit about it since we were all adults, and I really should be over the whole number one enemy from childhood thing, but...I'm a huge grudge holder, so I'm not getting over this anytime soon.

It doesn't help that the few times Hayes does come home, he flaunts his money and a new bimbo on his arm. Not that I would ever—and I mean ever—admit it out loud, but he is ridiculously attractive, to the point that I want to punch him in the balls just for being so insanely handsome.

No one should be that perfect on the outside and so ugly on the inside. Life can be so unfair sometimes.

"I'd rather you run me over with your car than touch Hayes."

"Dramatic. Whatever. It was just an idea. It's time to put yourself back out there, Soph. It's been over six months since HH. Can we please put you on the dating site? Just give it a shot. If it sucks, you can delete your profile."

"Dating sites are gross. A giant waste of time. I already tried it, and it was a shitshow. Everyone pretends to be someone they aren't just to match with someone. Remember that time I met the guy who brought his mother? He paid more attention to her than to me."

She squints her nose when she remembers that date. "Okay, true. But that was just one. You can't let one ruin it for them all."

"Okay...What about the guy who sucked his thumb...at thirty? Oh, or what about the one who recorded all our conversations so he could replay them later?"

"Alright. Fine. No dating sites. But, at least give your number to that guy from yoga. He was super hot."

I shake my head. "And he also likes the same guys that I do, Hol. Stop playing matchmaker. I'm fine being alone. Actually, I'm thriving being single, free, and happy with myself. Really."

"Whatever you say, Soph."

Okay, I'm lying. We both know it. I hate being alone. I prefer to be in a relationship, however comfortable it is, even if sex is scheduled. I'd choose that over waking up each morning alone.

"Fine. I'm lying."

"I know."

"One dating site. One. And not the Singles in Seattle one. That one was full of weirdos. Oh, what about this one?" I point to Tinder.

"Yes!" she squeals, clicking on the signup button. "You're going to meet the man of your dreams, just watch. When you least expect it, Mr. Perfect is going to sweep in and sweep you off your feet."

Famous last words, if there ever were any.

CHAPTER TWO

Hayes

"Sweetheart, don't be like that," I coo, amping up the charm that God has so graciously given me. Usually, I don't have to work this hard, but a woman scorned....

I duck just as a high heel sails past my head, barely missing, and hits the wall behind me with a loud thud.

"You're an asshole, Hayes!" the blonde from last night cries as she stomps around my penthouse, collecting her discarded scraps of clothing from various surfaces. Well, minus the heel she just tried to impale me with.

"I thought you knew what this was. I'm sorry, I'm not a relationship kinda guy," I mutter, my brow furrowed in confusion. We'd discussed this, in length—or at least I thought we had—before she'd dropped to her knees and made me forget my own name. This is why I rarely hook up outside of "the list". You know, the list that you call and faithfully, they answer. No drama, no attachments, no issues. This is what happens when you stray from the list. But sometimes the list is boring, and I'm a "live life on the edge" kinda guy. My dick is, at least.

Another shoe flies, and she screams in frustration as she snatches the pale pink lace bra from atop the lamp. I crouch down behind the leather chair in the far corner, safe from flying Louboutins, but the chair doesn't do much to block my six-foot-four, hockey-built body from her assault.

She's abandoning the shoes and moving on to my awards that sit on the bookshelf beside her.

Fantastic.

This gives new meaning to taking one for the team. You give a girl great dick, and they become mentally unstable.

One by one, the awards hit the wall behind my head, each one thrown with more oomph than the last, and the last one putting a hole in the drywall.

"Okay, Becca, let's talk about this." I peek from behind the chair to see her eyes drilling holes in my hiding spot.

"It's Beth! Jesus Hayes, you can't even get the name of the woman you sleep with right?!" she cries, chunking a vase this time, which hits the wall and shatters behind me.

I need to get this under control, and fast.

Listen, in my defense, there hadn't exactly been a lot of talking the night before, and when she decided to suck the soul out of my dick, I kind of lost all rational thought.

"I'm sorry! I was distracted. I can't help that there was a lot less talking than I expected."

"Whatever."

Now partially dressed, she pulls her purse up on her arm, and I take a chance and stand.

"Look, Beth," I pause, emphasizing the correct name, "I'm sorry I got your name wrong. I blame it on the alcohol, okay?" I give her my most charming grin, and she visibly softens before me.

"It's...It's fine. I just thought it would be different. Can I give you my number, you know, so you can call me sometime?" She trails off.

"Sure love, leave it with the doorman on your way out, yeah?" I drop a chaste kiss on her cheek and stroll off to the bathroom for a shower to wash last night off my body.

I hear a frustrated growl and the slam of the front door. Before I can even turn the water on to get in, my phone's ringing. I don't even have to look to know who it is, and I slide the bar to answer without looking.

Another day, another ass chewing.

"Kyle, my man, what's happening?" I grin when I hear my agent's dejected sigh.

"Did you at least check to make sure she hadn't stolen anything?"

I laugh, even though he's right. "I didn't, but don't worry, she spent most of the morning destroying the penthouse, so there wasn't much time left to steal anything."

"What?" he exclaims. I hear a car door shut, and he curses under his breath.

I can practically see the vein in his neck bulging as his face goes beet red. I've told him that shit isn't good for his health.

"Eh, she was a little angry that it wasn't more than a one night kind of thing."

"Hayes, did you at least have her sign the NDA? It's literally on your phone and takes two clicks. *Two*."

Fuck, I knew I forgot something. At least it wasn't the condom.

"Uh, I actually did not do that because I was a tad intoxicated."

"Listen, the league is breathing down my neck. You've got to get your shit under control, or you're going to forfeit the captain spot and find yourself without a team. I can only do so much damage control. This girl will be selling her story at the nearest tabloid in a heartbeat, and you know her version will be ten times worse than what actually happened. You're already out this year for your shoulder—do you really want to never return to NHL? Because that's what it fucking seems like. Continue like this and your hockey career is over."

"Kyle, I'm good. Just letting loose and trying to relax, okay?"

He sighs and doesn't respond. There's a beat of tense silence.

"Look, why don't I head home for a bit? Spend some time with Scott and the fam? I've got Gracie's birthday party coming up, and I can just stay a few days. Out of the tabloids. Give my shoulder time to heal," I say.

"I'll have Jess book the jet. Stay out of trouble, Hayes. You're on a thin rope that's ready to snap. I'll handle anything that happens with this girl, but for God's sake can you not sleep with any more puck bunnies before you leave?"

With that, he hangs up.

There are three things I love about going home to my tiny, barely-a-spot-on-the-map hometown—which, with one stoplight, a Main Street that leads into town, and only one way out, is the definition of the word "small-town":

1) Sunday mornings with Pops

2) My mama's cooking

3) Seeing my childhood best friend and his family

That's it.

The day I was drafted, I packed my bags and never looked back. There was nothing that Leavenworth could offer, so I took the first opportunity that presented itself. Hockey had always been in the cards, so it wasn't a surprise when the Wolves drafted me. I'm just lucky I'm only in Seattle rather than halfway across the country, where I couldn't see my parents often enough. Especially during the pre-season.

Mama calls every single Sunday without fail. I block that time out for her and wait faithfully for her phone call every week. It doesn't matter where I am or who I'm with—that time is hers. Call me what you want, but I'm a mama's boy, through and through.

I look up to see Mama's old, beat-up Ford pulling into the parking spot in front of me. That's one fight I'm never going to win.

The thing is older than I am, and it looks every bit of it. Mama loves that rusted heaper, and even though I could pay cash for a new Tahoe for her, she refuses, insisting that the truck is "perfectly fine and gets her where she needs to go." My dad and I have been on her for years to retire it, but she's not hearing any of it. And you don't argue with Mama.

Ma seems to be the only person in the world who truly doesn't care about the number of things she could have because her son is a pro hockey player. It's the reason a serious relationship is off the table for me. I never know if a woman is with me for what I can offer her or what she can make off of me.

"There's my baby!" she cries the second her foot hits the pavement, the heavily rusted door slamming shut behind her.

"Mama don't start fussing over me already." I grin, no conviction behind my words. I love when she fusses, but I can't say that. Wouldn't *dare* admit it. I'm not six-foot-four, built like a brick shit house, and the best defender in the country for nothing. I can't let anyone think I'm soft.

Truth is, I'm soft as fuck for Mama.

She rolls her eyes, pulling me to her. "Oh hush, you're my baby boy. I can fuss all I want, and you're not going to tell me a thing, Hayes."

"Yes ma'am." I give her a hug and let it linger for a moment, thankful that I decided to come home.

"How's your shoulder? Have you been taking it easy? I better not hear you've been on the ice, being rough."

Should have known she wasn't going to last five minutes without bringing it up. I'm still...adjusting to the fact that, for the first time in over fifteen years, I'm not going to be playing hockey this season. I've got a tear in my rotator cuff, and the doc says if I take time off, it'll likely heal on its own. But if I don't, the tear will get bigger and require surgery to fix it.

As small of a tear as it is, that motherfucker hurts.

I hate to sit on the sidelines and let my team down, but if I don't let this shoulder heal, chances are, surgery will be the end of my career.

So, here I am. Wondering what the fuck I'm going to do with the next year of my life.

"Ma, I'm good. I've been icing it. I can still skate, you know. My feet are fine. I just can't play an actual game and take the chance of someone hitting me. Don't worry."

Her eyes still pool with worry, but she smiles and pulls me back to her. "You've been gone too long. Let's get home—I have supper thawing, and your daddy will be excited to see you."

I nod and toss my bag into the bed of the truck with my good shoulder before hopping inside. The door creaks and grinds as it slams shut.

The drive through town is quiet—blissful in a way that can only be achieved in a place like this. It's serene and peaceful—the opposite of Seattle. Here, there are none of the city lights and no cars racing down the freeway to their next destination. It's exactly what I need after the week I've had.

"I saw you on the cover of one of those magazines, Hayes," Mama chides from the driver's seat.

I groan. "Mama, can we not?" I plead.

"Hayes, I'm just saying you're too old to be out there frolicking with these...women. It's time to settle down, find you a good woman, and give me some grandchildren."

And there it is.

There's nothing this woman wants more than to see me settled down and married off like my brothers and sisters.

Problem is, I've got no desire to settle down and get married or pop kids out.

I'm perfectly fine with how my life is.

"I'm good, Ma. Don't worry about me, okay? You need to worry about you and Dad. He said you went to the doctor this week for a heart scan. Everything go okay?"

She looks out the window, avoiding my eyes. "Everything is fine, Hayes. I would like to have some grandchildren before I die. Your old mama isn't getting any younger."

We ride the rest of the way home in silence, each of us looking out our own window.

Settling down is the last thing on my mind. Getting through the next year is the only part of the future I'm focused on.

CHAPTER THREE

Sophia

I hope whoever came up with the smart-ass idea to make giant, life-size unicorns into balloons stubs their big toe on the corner of their bed in the middle of the night...and gets an STD. Okay, a curable STD, but an STD all the same.

As usual, I'm fifteen minutes late to my godchild's birthday party, and now I'm wrestling the unicorn balloon out of the car, furthering my tardiness.

"For God's sake," I cry, yanking on the string and finally pulling the enormous thing free of the door.

Now I'm flustered and my hair is standing up in every direction because of the static from the balloon. And great, now it's sticking to the balloon. I'm trying to get my hair under control when I hear a soft chuckle and look up to see Hayes Davis strolling right past me, clutching a small, perfectly wrapped present with a bright pink bow.

That...*asshole*.

He saw me struggling with this stupid balloon, in heels, in the middle of a hot summer day, and he laughs and walks right past me like I'm not even here. If that doesn't describe who he is as a person, nothing will.

And Holly wonders why I hate him.

Aside from an ego that's so big I'm not sure how Holly's house will even begin to contain it, or the fact that he's arrogant and expects everyone to fall at his feet like he's some god or something?

Well, aside from that, it's most definitely the fact that he is so ridiculously good looking my stomach turns even looking at him.

Whatever. I don't need his help anyway.

I raise my chin higher, snatch the stupid unicorn balloon up, and stomp towards the front door. The party is already well on its way, and it does make me feel marginally better that Mr. Perfect is also late. The sound of children screaming and some princess soundtrack drift to the front yard, so I head through the side gate to the backyard. Just as I step onto the garden path, a shrill scream rings out, throwing me off balance. Before I can catch myself on, well anything, I feel my heel snap beneath my foot, and I'm going down.

I hit the ground, *hard*.

Really freaking hard.

Ugh.

The mulch from the landscaped path digs into my thighs as my dress hikes up, and my legs somehow end up tangled in the bundle of string attached to the ridiculous number of balloons I'm carrying. From my spot on the ground, I'm eye level with the crotch of the unicorn. Even better.

I glance down at my thrift store Louboutins and see that the spike of the heel is broken in half, and honestly, I don't think this moment can get any worse. I saved for exactly three months to buy these heels, and I feel the hot sting of tears well in my eyes.

"Uh...Sophia?"

The velvet voice comes from behind me. Without looking, I know exactly who it belongs to, and now I regret thinking that this moment couldn't get any worse...because it absolutely just did.

"I'm fine," I huff, tossing the spiked heel to the side and not-so-gracefully rising to my feet. With only one heel, I'm awkwardly uneven.

"Need some help, or...?" he asks from behind me again.

I turn to face him and give him the best scowl I can muster, "Nope."

His eyes, a vivid green I don't quite remember ever being that bright, do a slow, unashamed perusal of my body, then move back up, locking with mine. He smirks, and I want to kick him in the shin.

How could I forget how insanely irritating he can be without saying a single damn word? I don't wait for his smart-ass answer. Instead, I brush past him back towards the front of the house, hobbling on one heel.

I'm not sure if someone can actually die from embarrassment, but if so, I'd like to at least die in peace—without the hottest, most annoyingly arrogant player in the entire NHL getting front row seats.

Somehow, I make it to the front door and thrust it open, yanking in the bunch of balloons and toeing off my broken heel in the process. Holly's in the kitchen arranging food, and her eyes widen when she sees me stumble through the front door.

"Hoooooly shit, what the hell happened to you?" She grins and rushes over.

Thankfully, the stupid balloons are ripped from my white knuckles, and I can breathe without worrying that they'll trip me or blow away with the damn breeze.

"I just tripped, fell, and somehow broke my new Louboutins in the process. But I got the damn balloons."

She laughs at my exasperation, "Okay, well, glad you made it. Want a mimosa?"

"That would be fantastic, thank you." I follow her into the kitchen. Everything, and I do mean every literal surface, is pink and purple and somehow incorporated into a unicorn theme, and in this moment, I realize how unprepared for motherhood I am.

I am never going to be a Pinterest mom like Holly, and I am sure as shit not going to be the designated balloon girl from here on out. I refuse. I'll keep the cool aunt title and leave all the party planning and supply getting to Hol.

While she makes our mimosas, I glance out the window into the yard, watching as Gracie and her friends jump in the unicorn jump house they rented for the party, laughing and giggling. Scott's behind the grill with my arch nemesis, and most of the other dads are hovering nearby. It's the most domesticated thing I've ever seen—less Hayes, of course.

The guy doesn't have a selfless bone in his body. I'm surprised he doesn't have TMZ peeping over the fence for a photo or a puck bunny hanging off his arm. That's his usual MO, so I'm curious as to why he's here sans bleach blonde with too little clothes.

He definitely has a type—that much is apparent.

"Soph?" Holly's voice makes me tear my eyes from Hayes.

"What'd you say? Sorry."

She gives me a knowing look, "So, I see you've seen Hayes."

"Briefly. Still as arrogant and pompous as always."

Before she can answer, the back door flies open, followed by, "Mommmmyyyy!!!"

My godchild runs in with tears streaming down her face and collapses into a fit at her mother's feet, and I have to bite my lip to keep from laughing. It's the most dramatic thing I've ever seen. Holly mouths "drama" before scooping Gracie up off the floor, drying the crocodile tears from her cheeks.

"What's wrong, baby?"

"Daddy says we can't open p-presents until after cake." She sags against Holly's chest as she wails.

"Well, sweetie, that's how birthdays go."

Gracie pauses, thinking about what Holly has said and then responds, "Uncle Hayes says it's my birthday, and that means I can do whatever I want."

My eyebrows shoot up.

"Did he?" Holly asks.

"He did, and he even said that it's my birthday and I can cry about it if I want to. Daddy used the 'shut up' word though."

"How about you go outside, and Mommy will be there in just a few minutes. Then we'll go ahead and eat your yummy unicorn cake and open presents, okay?"

A few more tears, some grumbling, and a handful of dramatic wails later, Gracie finally feels okay enough to rejoin her friends outside. The second she's surrounded, the dramatics of her tears are gone, the redness of her cheeks the only sign that it even happened.

"Wow," I breathe, laughing.

"Tell me about it. Every day is a new drama with that one."

She thrusts a mimosa at me, and I accept the glass, taking a hefty sip.

Ninety percent champagne, ten percent orange juice. Just how I like it. And after the fiasco of even getting here, I need the alcohol more than ever. Especially when I'm going to be subjected to being around Hayes for the remainder of the afternoon.

"Alright, let's get out there before my husband starts a fight club for kids."

"What's sad is I can one hundred percent see that happening. My money's on Gracie though—that girl's got a badass right hook."

Holly laughs as she slides the cake off the counter. The cake is a full-size unicorn, sparkly golden horn and all, and it looks to be enough to feed at least fifty people, easily.

"Can you get the door for me? This thing weighs a shit ton," she grunts, while the cake wobbles in her arms.

I hold the door open, and she walks through slowly. When the kids realize she's carrying a cake, they start screaming, and suddenly she's got an entire daycare in front of her.

My eyes flick against my will to Hayes. The arms of his fitted black t-shirt hug his biceps as if they'll bust like a can of biscuits at any moment. Of course, I would compare the world's hottest hockey player's biceps to a can of biscuits.

No wonder I'm single.

With the swarm of kids surrounding Holly, Scott, and Gracie—along with their parents—that leaves me and Hayes hanging back in the kid-less section. Being around him is inevitable, so I suck it up, like always.

I attempt to be the bigger person. "Attempt" being the key word. It's next to impossible standing next to the six-foot hockey devil in khakis.

"St. James, you're looking especially annoyed today," he sing-songs from beside me. I glance up to shoot him a death stare, and the teasing grin on his lips only widens when he sees the annoyance on my face. He lives for this shit.

"How many times have I told you not to call me that? I've honestly lost track. We're no longer in elementary school, Hayes. The nicknames are childish."

I fold my arms over my chest and drag my eyes from his, focusing on Gracie as she and her friends "ooh" and "aah" at the

33

monstrosity of a cake in front of her. At least she's amused. I'm hyper aware of Hayes standing only inches apart from me, but I refuse to meet his eyes, clenching my jaw in disdain and feigning boredom instead.

"Aww, don't be like that, St. James. What can I say? The name just stuck. Plus, how many times have I told you I'm going to do the exact opposite of what you want?"

Add his ability to unnerve me with just his childlike ridicule to the list of things I loathe about him. It's something he obviously hasn't grown out of over time. Unlike most males, who leave the immaturity in high school, Hayes just seems to have gotten worse in adulthood.

"Pity, I was hoping you'd be preoccupied with a puck bunny today, but I obviously can't be that lucky," I retort. I force my eyes to stay on the birthday cake, as much as my traitorous body would love for me to look at him. I won't give him the satisfaction.

He scoffs, "Eh, she had to get her lips done or some shit."

Fitting.

Before I can respond, Scott is walking up with a curious look on his face. "What are you two arguing about now?'

My eyebrows raise, and I offer a noncommittal shrug. "Oh, just letting Hayes know that his ego has officially reached astronomical size, in case he hadn't noticed."

I smirk at Scott, and he laughs lowly, shaking his head.

"You just missed it. I was telling Tits there's more to life than Tinder and guys who can only last thirty seconds," Hayes says, his tone proud, as if he's gotten the last word in.

My jaw drops before I can stop my reaction. *Asshole.*

"I swear, I wish you two would just bang this shit out and move on." Scott laughs and turns to clean the grill with his wire brush, giving us his back.

"I wouldn't touch him with a ten-foot pole, and that's being gracious," I respond, shooting a 'ha' smirk at Hayes, who returns his own.

"Don't worry St. James, the feeling is mutual. I like my women... not insane."

I hate him. Actually, "hate" isn't a strong enough word. I loathe his very existence. In the midst of our back and forth arguing, we've clearly missed singing "Happy Birthday", because Holly yells, "Who wants cake?" And the kids go wild.

She cuts squares and begins passing them out to everyone, and even though it is the most over the top cake I've ever seen, it *does* look delicious.

Just what I need after dealing with Hayes.

Of course, we both reach for the same plate. I tug it towards me with a sneer, "Can you not?"

His eyebrows raise, "Pretty sure I grabbed it first, St. James."

I yank it towards me, and he yanks it back to him, and we go back and forth, each of us shooting daggers at the other.

Then, he suddenly lets go, and the plate goes flying, sending the enormous piece of cake ...directly onto my face.

It lands with a splat, and bright pink and purple icing coat my face, eyelashes, and mouth.

That's it, I am going to fucking kill him.

"Shit," I hear him mutter, and I snatch another plate of cake off the table. I run towards him, full force, and slap him in the face with it.

There's a shocked gasp, and a few whistles, but right now I'm so angry and embarrassed that I don't even care.

"You did not just do that," he grits, slinging some of the cake off his face.

"Sure as shit did. Asshole."

"Both of you, stop." Holly hands us both napkins. "Go inside and get cleaned up. This is a birthday party, for fuck's sake."

Shit, I was so caught up in the moment I didn't even think about all of the kids seeing that.

"Fine," I mutter and spin on my heel, stomping inside.

I hear his footsteps and know he's trailing behind me. Moving to the kitchen sink, I grab a towel and am cleaning the cake off of my face when I hear him scoff behind me. I whip around, prepared to tell him exactly what the hell I think about him, when he moves to stand in front of me, so close my heart falls to my butt.

"What are you doing?" I murmur.

He's entirely too close, and my body is reacting in traitorous ways.

Damnit.

He cages me in, icing still smeared on his cheeks and lips, then leans down closer to me. "You wanna play games, St. James?"

I can feel his breath against my lips, and it sends a shiver down my spine. Why the hell does it feel so good to have him pressed against me?

He's the enemy, and my hormones are currently making me into a traitor.

"I don't want anything to do with you, actually. But your ego makes that hard to see, huh?"

He laughs, so low and hoarse I feel it in my stomach. "I think you want a war, and baby...I play to win."

He presses further against me, and unless I've totally lost my mind—which very well may be—he's hard against my stomach. He leans down closer and closer until I think he might kiss me, but the back door flies open, and Scott walks in, making us break apart like we've been caught with our hands down the other's pants.

"Uh, time for presents?" Scott says, eying us both warily.

"Coming. Just getting the cake off my face, thanks to your asshole best friend," I mutter.

Hayes laughs, grabbing the towel from my hands and wiping his face clean before tossing it back at my face and walking out the door.

I loathe this man.

When I walk back outside, the kids are gathered around Gracie, faces full of cake and amped up on sugar. Their screams are deafening, and my ears pop with the sheer intensity of it.

Wow, never underestimate five-year-olds and their ability to raise the roof.

Gracie is eating up being the center of attention. My godchild is so much like her mother, it's scary.

I continue ignoring Hayes, folding my arms across my chest and desperately trying to forget...whatever it is that just passed between us in the house. Holly begins handing Gracie presents, finally getting to my bright pink wrapped present.

Look, I might not be the most maternal person on the planet, but I do know my godchild, and she's obsessed with Barbies and DreamHouses. So, being the best godmother on the planet, I got her her very first Barbie DreamHouse, complete with a Ken doll and Barbie convertible, and I'm ninety-nine percent positive that nobody can top this gift.

Gracie tears into the paper like a wild animal. When she sees the house, her jaw gapes, and her eyes go wide as saucers.

"Aunt SOPHHHHHIE!" she screams, then runs over and hits me like a linebacker with a hug. "Thank you thank you thank you!"

I give her a quick kiss and usher her back over to the table, where she waits for the next presents from her mom.

Using this ample opportunity, I shoot a smirk at Hayes, who looks annoyed. Ha! He might have more money than everyone at this party combined, but nobody knows Gracie like I do.

She goes through the presents in record time, until she's at her very last box.

"Okay Gracie Pie, this is it. Looks like it's from Uncle Hayes." Holly hands her a medium-sized box I saw Hayes carrying into the party earlier while I dealt with the balloon fiasco.

Her tiny hands tear through the paper, and once she's gotten it off the top, she screams so loudly I'm sure she's going to bust someone's eardrum, "An iPad! Uncle Hayes, oh my god!!!"

She runs to him, and he catches her, swinging her off the ground, suddenly my girl's hero.

"This is the best birthday present ever!" she cries, throwing her arms around his neck.

"Well, I guess I shouldn't mention the brand new bike I parked out front? The one with the pink tassels that you sent me a picture of?"

I all but scoff at his tone. Of course he'd try to one-up me at our goddaughter's birthday party. Typical Hayes. He's always got to be the best in the room. I just got one-upped by the douchebag pro athlete with pink tassels.

Damnit.

Remember that ego I mentioned? He's arrogant and self-centered, and it only makes me hate him more.

I slap on a fake, strained smile when she squeals and runs out front, the herd of children following her.

"You ass," I spit, stepping into his space until we're toe to toe.

He grins, shrugging his shoulders, "What can I say, Uncle Hayes always delivers." His words drip with innuendo, and I want to punch him square in the face. If we weren't at our goddaughter's birthday party, I would. Right now, I'd much rather knee him in the dick, but as it is, I can't imagine that going over well with Scott and Hol.

"Be a doll and bring this inside." Hayes thrusts the empty bowl that held the meat for the grill into my arms and strides past me over to Gracie, where he takes her into his arms and swings her around. For someone so annoying, he's good with kids.

I consider chunking the bowl at his head but think twice when I look up to see Holly eyeing me. Something tells me that if I missed and somehow hit the glass on the back patio, Holly would not be so forgiving.

Fine.

Sucking in a deep, semi-calming breath, I walk inside to put the bowl in the dishwasher.

Only a little while longer, I tell myself. Thirty minutes—an hour tops—and Hayes will be back on his private jet, heading back to the life of the rich and famous, and I won't have to be around him. I'm sure his face will grace the cover of the tabloids, since he can't seem to stay out of trouble for the life of him, but I can shut it off and pretend he doesn't even exist.

Or so I keep telling myself.

Maybe one of these days I'll actually believe it.

THE ENEMY TRAP

CHAPTER FOUR

Hayes

Two days later, Sophia St. James *still* invades my thoughts. It had been a while since I'd seen her, and I'd forgotten how attractive she is. How....annoying she is. Surprisingly, the two go hand in hand when Sophia's involved. It seems like her distaste for me has only grown in the time we've been apart. Fine with me. I'll gladly play my part in the game she has set for us both.

My mind fills again with the image of Sophia at the birthday party, her fists clenched by her sides as she glares at me. Such a little thing to be so full of fury. Fuck, she's so tiny I could throw her over my shoulder without even breaking a sweat.

That long blonde hair of hers just calls for my fist. I groan inwardly, and my thoughts shift to her ass and how it's not okay how good it looked in those jeans. What? I'm a guy—so sue me. And the second she'd opened her mouth? I groan again. I'd forgotten completely about those round, plump...

"You need another beer Hayes?" Scott's question interrupts my musing. I shake my head to rid myself of any and all thoughts of St. James.

"Nah, I'm still working on this one. Thanks, though." I hold my beer up to show Scott the half-full bottle.

He walks back into the kitchen while I sit in front of the massive round table he's set up outside on their patio. "Guy's night" is officially in full swing. He'd shipped the tiny terrors off to his parents, given Holly the boot—to St. James's I'm sure—and now poker night is about to start. A few of our friends from high school are headed over, and that's the thing I love about coming home. While hockey dominates my life in more than one aspect, I can always come home and know that the guys won't treat me any differently, and I'll always have a place here for poker night. With my schedule and the social shit my agent schedules for me, these days are few and far between. I miss the simplicity of my hometown, but not enough to ever come back permanently.

"Guys should be here soon." Scott flops down into the chair next to me and swipes the old deck of cards off the table—the same deck we've had since senior year. The corners are worn and yellowed from over ten years of use. We used to sneak into his parents' basement in high school and bet away our life savings after a hockey game. Scott's a sentimental asshole like that. He's never been one to let go of the past.

"So, how's celebrity life?"

I roll my eyes and scoff, "Kyle's on my ass worse than ever. Says

I've gotta get my shit together before the league drops me."

Scott nods and takes a long pull from his beer, peering out into the back yard. He's silent for a moment before he speaks. I can practically see the wheels turning in my best friend's head. I've known him long enough to know him better than anyone.

"You've been on the pages a lot, Hayes. The fuck's going on with you? You're out there chasing puck bunnies like we're in college again. Dude, we're almost thirty."

I'd known this was coming, but it didn't lessen the blow of his words.

"I'm just having fun, man. Partying it up before I'm tied down like you, signing my life away to someone. Seems like everyone here is married off and popping out kids, and the thought alone makes me break out in hives. I'm not cut out for that shit."

"I get it. But stop thinking of marriage as a death sentence. Holly and the kids are the best thing to ever happen to me. I wouldn't trade it for anything, especially not chasing after some puck bunnies who only want you for what you can give them. C'mon man. I'm just worried about you. Holly's worried about you. Especially with the shit with your shoulder. You're not getting any younger, man. You've gotta start taking care of yourself." His gaze burns into me, hitting me at a soft spot in my chest in a way I wasn't prepared for.

Aside from my parents, Scott,Holly, and their kids are the closest thing I have to family, and I fucking hate that I'm disappointing them.

"I'm good. I'm reining it in. Kyle's already given me a lecture. No more puck bunnies, no more partying. I've been resting, elevating my shoulder, and doing the exercises he gave me. It'll be alright." I tear my gaze from his and take a pull from my beer, letting the amber liquid slide down my throat as a distraction.

"Well, since you're turning your life around and all, I've got a favor."

I look back at him, and he's got a shit-eating grin. Before he even makes his request, I know I'm in for it. Fucker pulled me in with the disappointment lecture.

"Hit me."

"Holly needs someone to do a styled shoot for a big vendor that's interested in working with her. They do custom wedding gowns and tuxedos. It would be an easy hour-long shoot, and you'll get good press from it. And we all know how good you look in a suit—cheeks of steel."

"Shit, Scott, anything else. I'll be your pool boy. I'll cut your grass. Need a date night? I'll babysit."

He knows how much I detest being on camera, seeing as how the damn things are constantly being pointed at me, capturing every aspect of my life. It just so happens that Holly's a photographer. Thankfully, she does mostly family stuff, but apparently, she's branching out.

"An hour. Tops. You need to be on camera doing something besides getting caught with a bunny, literally and figuratively, for once."

"You know we don't bring up the sex tape."

He shrugs, his eyebrows raising as a grin tugs at the corner of his lips, "Gonna bring it up unless you say yes."

"Fuck." I groan, dropping my head back.

He had me. Hook, line, and sinker.

"Fine. But you're talking to Kyle about it. I've had enough ass chewing for the month."

"Already did."

Great.

He offers up no other information as our friends walk through the French doors, whooping and hollering, slapping my back, and talking stats. I don't know what the hell I just signed myself up for.

CHAPTER FIVE
Sophia

" I cannot believe I let you talk me into this. Seriously...I can't believe I'm actually here. " I groan.

"Stop talking and suck it in so she can tighten it," Holly chastises me, all while grinning when I have the air ripped from my lungs by a twenty-something dress assistant as she yanks on the strings of the too-tight corset. Somehow, Holly has talked me into doing a "styled shoot" with her for a new vendor she is desperately trying to work with. Her "go to" models weren't available, and the vendor asked last minute to make this happen.

It took lots of wine and even more guilt tripping, but now... here I am. I love my best friend, I do. It's just that sometimes I want to punch her for all the ideas she has that I get roped into. I'm always her guinea pig.

"Remind me exactly why I agreed to this, again?"

My eyes drag down the floor length mirror in front of me. There are four panes of glass that line the walls, showcasing the room. As if it needed to look any more inviting, being tucked away inside a yacht that costs more money than I will ever probably see in my lifetime. My stomach tightens at how much money this thing actually costs—or how much this dress that I'm currently not breathing to fit inside costs.

Apparently, the vendor Holly is working with wanted a seaside-styled wedding shoot featuring this yacht. It all seems so grandiose to me, but I can see in Holly's eyes how much this means to her, so I'm putty in her well-played hands.

And let's be real, what else do I have to do? I've been at home in my pajamas, eating ice cream on the couch and binge-watching *New Girl*. Such an exciting life I live.

"Because you're my best friend and you love me," she singsongs, doing a whirl around the spacious room below deck and sighing when she sees the ceiling lined with mirrors as well. "We totally have to do some shots in this room. It screams 'wild and uninhibited.'"

My eyebrows furrow with genuine confusion, "It does? Speaking of...Where is this groom I'm supposed to be photographed with?"

Her eyes dart to mine, and she busies herself with her camera. "So, we're going to go ahead and sail out, and he'll meet us there in a smaller boat. There was a small hang up, and we still have to finish getting you ready anyway."

"Ooooookay," I quip, the assistant pulling even tighter on the corset strings. As much as I feel like I'm stuffed into this size four, as I eye myself in the mirror, I can't help but notice how it flatters my body. It's tight as a glove and definitely constricting my breathing, but it hugs my hips in all the right places. It's a mermaid fit, so my hips are prominent and my waist tiny from the corset.

"You look hot as fuck," Holly breathes, her eyes lighting up. "This is going to be awesome!"

The assistant behind me gives her a look but scurries off without another word. Suddenly, the yacht lurches, and I realize we must be moving.

"And we're off!"

My stomach turns, partially from the dress and partially from the sudden rocking of the boat. Even what I'm sure is a million-dollar yacht isn't beyond the uneven movements of a boat as it heads out to sea.

"Now, time for makeup," Holly says, holding up the oversized sack of makeup she's brought from home.

"Joy," I mutter, then fall into the chair she's graciously moved behind me. The movement is awkward and more of a flop, since I can't exactly bend at the waist. Every second I spend in this room below deck, I'm getting more nervous and anxious about this shoot with a stranger.

Holly spends the next 20 minutes or so putting makeup on me, and when she's done and turns me to face the mirrors, my jaw drops. I look...beautiful. For the first time since I had my heart broken and ripped to pieces, I feel like myself. My eyes are bright blue, vibrant under the neutral shadows on my eyelids. They're framed with the thick, black lashes she's glued on, making me look demure and seductive without even trying. I'm shocked.

"Holy shit, Soph, you look amazing. The dress, the makeup, the hair. All of it."

I swallow thickly, forcing down the body shaming retort that threatens to spill from my lips out of habit—a habit I only recently seem to have formed. I no longer felt good enough, for myself or anyone else. That's why men cheat, right? Because they find a younger, hotter version that you'll never be.

"Soph?" Holly says, breaking through my thoughts.

"Yeah, sorry. I was in my head. It looks amazing, Hol, thank you."

My voice is sincere, and tears threaten to spill over my freshly made-up face. *Breathe, Soph, now is not the time to lose your shit.*

"Okay, so we should be getting close to our destination. I'm going to go up and check in. Stay here, and I'll be right back!"

Seconds later, she's gone, up the winding stairs that lead to the deck. Well, okay. Once I'm alone, I look around the room she's left me in. It's obviously the master suite of the yacht and coincidentally bigger than my entire apartment. Okay, maybe not, but it definitely comes close. The mirrors on the ceiling do give it a certain...vibe. It seems like the perfect place for hot, sweaty sex now that I think about it.

Too bad it's me and Bob for life. He's not all that bad, but I think it may be time for an upgrade.

I hear shuffling on the deck, followed by the sound of an engine. It must be my groom to be arriving, and whoever dropped him off leaving. I pick my phone up from the nearby table and open social media, scrolling and waiting patiently for Holly to come back and help me up the stairs in this monstrous dress.

Five minutes turns into ten...then twenty, and then forty minutes. My back aches from the awkward position I've been in, so I stand and stretch my arms.

Where is Holly? It's been forever.

I walk around the room, thankful that the dress seems to have stretched ever so slightly in the forty minutes I was sitting. I can breathe just a tiny bit easier now. I trail my fingers over the satin sheets on the bed. Holy shit, sleeping on that would be like sleeping on a cloud of cotton. I make it to the stairs and peer up at the cracked door above.

Fuck it. I've been down here forever. Gathering the train of the dress, I pull the stilettoes off my feet, toss them to the ground next to the stairs, and slowly make my way up each step. The dress is so tight around my legs I can hardly step up with each ascending stair.

Jesus, how do people wear these dresses? I can't imagine getting married in front of hundreds of people and having to be stuffed into this thing for hours. Talk about a literal can of busted biscuits, because the second my ass tried to drop it like it was hot on that dance floor, everyone would get a view of these biscuits. Literally.

I finally make it to the door and thrust it open, almost losing my footing, but thankfully righting myself just before I fall against the wall. The sun is bright and beaming down. I feel its warm kiss on the tops of my shoulders, which are on full display. I don't see anyone on deck—not Holly, not a captain...no one. It looks almost...deserted.

Now I'm nervous. Did something happen? Were we pirated? My mind immediately flashes to Pirates of the Caribbean and a delicious Johnny Depp, and then I realize how utterly ridiculous that sounds. But as I walk across the wooden deck, I see no one.

What the hell? Where is Holly?

A noise behind me makes me whip around, as quick as I can in this sheath, that is, and to my absolute surprise, I'm face to face with Hayes. Who just so happens to be wearing a tux that seems like it was designed perfectly to fit his body.

Then, it dawns on me. He looks just as surprised to see me.

Oh no. Oh no no no no.

I groan before cutting him with my eyes, "Please tell me that Holly did not talk you into this and that somehow you just ended up on the wrong boat."

His handsome face erupts into a look of confusion, "No...but Scott did."

Great. This is just great.

I leave Hayes standing there to search the rest of the boat, and low and behold it is deserted. Not a passenger in sight, except myself and the person I may just end up pushing overboard and pretending he was never here in the first place.

Hayes walks up as I flop onto the outer deck bench and run my hands through my hair.

"What's going on? Where is the photographer?" he asks me.

I look up at him, determined not to let my eyes drift down his body to see the way his tailored suit hugs every muscle in a way that should honestly be illegal.

I refuse.

"There is no photographer, Hayes." I mutter. I can't believe I let her ass talk me into this, only to have her pull one over on us both. Easily.

"What do you mean?"

He looks out at the ocean surrounding us, and there's nothing in sight. We're so far out to sea that you can't even see the shoreline. The wind kicks up, and I see a piece of paper taped to the cockpit, blowing with the breeze.

I walk over to it and rip it off, recognizing Holly's messy scrawl.

Soph & Hayes,

By now, you've probably realized that you're stuck. Together. On this yacht. For the next twenty-four hours.

Call it...intuition, but Scott and I both realize that you two have "something" to work through, and being the great friends that we are... we pushed it along.

Don't worry: You're anchored in a safe spot (sorry, but no keys), and there's enough food and water for a week. Lots of wine and bourbon too.

We'll see you tomorrow night, and hopefully by then you two have talked—or made use of those mirrors—and we can all breathe easier.

Sorry, but not sorry at all.

XOXO Holly and Scott.

Oh my god. When I get off this boat, I am going to murder her. Literally, I'm going to kill her. Lifelong friendship right down the drain.

This is ten times worse than what I thought.

Trapped on a yacht in the middle of the ocean with...Hayes?

I shove the letter into his chest and brush past him to create as much space as I can between us.

"Well, Hayes, I know your brain is small and somewhat damaged from all of the hits you've taken, but it looks like our friends just parent-trapped us."

His brow furrows in confusion, "They what?" he asks, before scanning the now crumpled letter from our no good, backstabbing friends.

"Goddamnit," he mutters, crumpling the letter and tossing it in front of him.

"Don't worry; I'm just as excited as you are."

I'd rather be face to face with my cheating, asshole ex-fiancé than be stuck on this boat with Hayes and his astronomical ego. The thought makes my stomach clench. And because I'm currently avoiding emotions, I'm not ready to decipher what that means.

"I *knew* he was up to something. Damnit," he says, undoing the bowtie at his neck with fervor and flopping down onto the bench seat I just stood from.

"So, what...are we just stranded here?" I screech, the harsh reality of our situation settling over me.

"What would you like me to do, St. James? They have the keys, and I have no phone. What about you?"

My eyes widen when it dawns on me that my phone is on 2% from my forty-five minutes of scrolling and the fact that I passed out on the couch after my wine, ice cream, and *New Girl* binge last night.

Damnit.

"It's dead."

He scoffs, "Of course it is. Looks like we're stuck for the next twenty-four hours, and unless you wanna hop over the side and swim your way to shore, we're not going anywhere." He clenches his jaw, and I watch the muscles tighten as he grits his teeth together. Obviously, Hayes wants nothing to do with me, and the feeling is mutual.

"No, but I'd love to shove you overboard and spend the next twenty-four hours sunbathing and drinking wine. Don't tempt me."

"Right, see how far you get in that dress. What did they do, paint it on you?" His eyes drag down my body in a slow perusal. I don't see a hint of appreciation...mostly just annoyance.

Screw him. I look damn good in this dress. I know his taste is more...classless.

"Right, I forget seeing a woman in a wedding dress opposite you is what, like your biggest fear? Scared of commitment and all of that, right Hayes? The great Hayes Davis, too scared to do anything but shove his hockey stick into puck bunnies."

His eyes harden, "Keeping up with me, St. James? You seem to know a lot about my life for claiming to hate me as much as you do."

I stand abruptly, finished with the bickering between us. My nerves are shot, and now that I'm actually not going to be using this dress, I need out of it.

The sun is beginning to set, and my stomach rumbles as if on a timer, reminding me that I haven't eaten anything since lunch. If I'm going to get off this boat without losing my mind or going to prison for murder, I need all the wine I can get my hands on.

"Going so soon?" Hayes quips, rising as I do and walking over to stand toe to toe with me. He towers over me, and I have to crane my neck to see him. The height difference between us is ridiculous—not that I had never noticed prior to now.

"Anywhere that you aren't. It's a big yacht. I'm sure there's plenty of room for us to completely avoid each other." I cross my arms, and his eyes drop to my chest for a brief moment before he drags them back to stare into my eyes.

"Do what you want, St. James, but I'm getting drunk. Going to have to since I've got to deal with you for the next twenty-four hours."

He brushes past me, leaving me standing on the deck with my mouth agape. Oh, to deal with me?

I'm seething. Starving. And out of options.

Whether I like it or not, I'm stuck with Hayes for the next

twenty-four hours, unless I wanted to risk getting eaten by a shark and attempt to swim back to shore.

Which might not be that bad of an idea at this point....

CHAPTER SIX

Hayes

Fuck *me.*

Worst case scenario is me in the same room as Sophia for an extended period of time. This?

Stranded in the middle of the goddamn ocean for the next twenty-four hours?

Catastrophic.

Fuck. I drag my hand down my face in frustration as I go in search of a bottle of bourbon. I need a drink, and I need off this damn boat. I need a damn ocean *between* Sophia St. James and me. I find the kitchen below deck through the door that she apparently just emerged from. Taking a look through the rooms, I see a decent-sized kitchen, a massive bedroom, and a bathroom—complete with a shower that's the size of most small bedrooms. In different circumstances, I'd enjoy being stranded on a yacht like this, but as it happens, I'm stranded with a thorn the size of Canada poking into my side.

The mouth on her. Every time she opens it, I have to clench my fists at my side so I don't throw her over my lap and spank her ass until it's as red as her face gets when she's angry. Infuriating, hard-headed, stubborn woman. She has enough attitude to last a fucking lifetime, and she can't open her mouth without trying to piss me off with a low blow.

Whatever her issue is with me, it has only gotten worse over time.

I find the bourbon on a shelf right next to the stainless steel fridge. The crystal canister has glasses neatly placed next to it, and I can't pour it fast enough. I pour two fingers and throw them back, not bothering to savor the flavor.

I wasn't kidding when I said the only way we're both making it off this boat is if I can drink myself to sleep so I don't have to listen to her mouth. If not, I'm surely going to throw her ass overboard for fish food.

Fuck, now I'm picturing her ass in that dress. It hugs her body so tightly I can make out the two dimples at the base of her spine, right above the delectable globes that I want to sink my teeth into. After I spank the attitude out of her.

The door slamming behind me thankfully interrupts my train of thought. And here comes Sophia, stomping towards me.

"Look, let's make this as pain free and easy as possible. You stay on your side of the boat, and I'll stay on mine."

I grin and toss back another two fingers of bourbon, letting the burn resonate this time. "Gonna be a little hard to do that, St.

James. Only one bed." I nod towards the bed beside her. Her eyes dart to the bed and back to me twice before she speaks.

"Hell no. You're sleeping on the floor."

"Who said anything about sleeping?" I ask.

She screeches before grabbing the closest thing to her, which happens to be a curling iron, and chunking it at my head. I duck in the nick of time, and it falls to the floor behind me with a loud clank.

"Hmm, might wanna work on your aim. A little too far to the left. I'm good with making it into tight holes; want a lesson?" I grin and brush past her.

"Just stay the hell out of my way, Hayes. Go upstairs and do... anything but annoy me."

I don't respond, climbing the stairs that lead back to the deck and letting the door slam shut behind me.

"Oh my god, you are ridiculous. That is not the Little Dipper, that's a damn airplane, Hayes. It's blinking!" Sophia cries, collapsing into a fit of drunken giggles next to me on the upper deck as we watch the stars.

How we got here...well, let's just say once the liquor started to flow, Sophia St. James became a woman I'd never met. Fun, uninhibited, carefree. I had to catch her before she went overboard when a wave hit while she stood too close to the side.

"You need your eyes checked, St. James. That is a fucking star."

Her eyes roll, and she drops back down from her elbows to her back while she stares at a sky that's bright with stars.

"I hate you a little less right now," she whispers, her voice so low I almost don't hear her.

I scoff, not taking my eyes off the view, even though I'm desperate to see her eyes, "And that brings me to one of the burning questions I've been dying to know the answer to for the past ten years. Why does Sophia St. James hate me in the first place?"

"You're a man-whore, and you're single-handedly responsible for my low self-esteem in high school."

"Me?" I ask, sitting up. Her blonde hair falls in wisps around her face, free from the curly updo that she started with. She's fucking gorgeous, even if she's the most annoying woman I've ever met. Right now, drunk as a fucking skunk, she's...tolerable.

For now.

It's her turn to scoff, "Psh, like you don't remember. Can we not go down memory lane? I'd rather throw myself into the ocean. Thanks." She rises, wobbling, and I have to reach my hand out to steady her. My hand grips her thigh, and a shiver runs down my spine as her soft, milky flesh is splayed beneath my hand. So tiny. Fun sized, minus the fun.

When she freezes under my touch, I clear my throat and drop my hand from her skin, then stand.

"I think we need more shots," I tell her, grinning.

She nods her head, "Yessss, and music."

That's how we end up below deck with the yacht's surround sound vibrating through the massive speakers. My first mistake was letting Sophia choose the music. We've been listening to nineties hits for the past thirty minutes. I've claimed a chair at the dining table while I watched her hips sway with the beat of alternative rock.

"I fucking love this song," she says, clutching an invisible microphone. Great, another Backstreet Boys serenade.

I can't help the laugh that escapes—she looks absurd singing into a microphone made of air, like she's center stage in a sold-out arena.

"Get up, come dance, c'mon."

"Absolutely not, St. James. The show's perfect from right here in this chair."

Her cheeks warm with my compliment. Truth is, if I stand from this chair, I'm going to lace my hands in her long, honey locks, pull her to me, and kiss her until she can't fucking breathe.

Call it what you want. Maybe it's the liquor that courses through my veins, or the dips of her hips that beg for bad decisions, but I've been sitting in this chair with a hard on for the past thirty minutes. With each shot we take, I find her less annoying and more attractive. Actually, that's a lie. She's always been fucking gorgeous. But without her attitude, I find myself more attracted to her than I've ever been.

"Fine. Your loss." She sings along to another boy band while I chuckle, sipping on my drink. Thunder claps in the distance, and the yacht lurches seconds later, just before the power goes out.

Sophia shrieks and darts towards me, jumping into my lap. Her arms fly to my neck, where she clutches on for dear life. Drunk Sophia is a carefree Sophia.

"What the fuck," she whispers.

I laugh. "Storm's coming. We're on a yacht, St. James. What do you expect? Generator will kick on in a minute."

Her eyes, deep blue pools, are wide as they stare back into mine. The air in the room shifts, and it isn't because of the storm outside. There's a storm brewing in this room, and the way that her fingers absentmindedly run through the hair at the nape of my neck does nothing but push me further and further toward the edge that we're dangling over. An edge we have no business walking on.

The tension is palpable. I want to grab hold of it, manipulate it, and make it—make her— fucking mine, right now. Tequila or not; doesn't matter. My heart speeds up in my chest at the thought of having her beneath me, squirming with desire.

The last thing Sophia and I need is something messy that has no way to be repaired. We share best friends and godchildren, and we have lives that are entangled. We don't need another reason to hate each other. Or yet another reason to make things weird when we're forced to be around each other.

Right now, I don't hate Sophia St. James and her mouth at all. Instead, I want it wrapped around my dick, her plump, pink lips in a perfect O shape as she takes me down her throat.

God bless America.

I know she can feel how hard I am, but I don't give one shit right now. I'm lost in her ocean eyes. I'm in the middle of the ocean with the girl who is my enemy, and now I want her, and I don't care about the aftermath or the consequences.

"Hayes..." Her tone is a warning, firm, yet not at all. There's not a hint of conviction in her words. It's a warning that she's just as far gone as I am. Because this isn't what either of us would really want if we were sober.

Is that the truth though? Would I no longer want St. James if I didn't have an entire bottle of bourbon in my system?

I place my hands on her small waist and pick her up, setting her on her feet.

"I'm going to check outside and make sure everything's good."

She nods, biting the inside of her cheek but saying nothing. I feel her eyes on me as I walk up the stairs and, only once the door slams behind me do I feel the tension dissolve.

Jesus, Hayes. Calm the fuck down. This shit is exactly what Holly and Scott wanted, and I refuse to give them the satisfaction after the sneaky shit they pulled to get us here.

Once I'm outside, the sideways rain assaults me the second I open the door. The wind is blowing so hard I have to hold on to the railing so I don't lose my footing on the slick, rain-soaked deck.

Woah.

It's so dark I can't see much around the yacht, but the thunder claps and lightning lights up the sky. All I can see for miles is pitch black. The waves are rocking and sloshing back and forth, pulling the boat in different directions. It's a bad storm, but not one that would require me to call in on the radio.

I've been sailing since I was a kid. I can handle this. If, for one second, I didn't think that I could, I'd turn us to shore, but part of me wants to wait the night out and see where it takes us. For whatever reason. I'm blaming it on the level of intoxicated I am, and not at all on the fact that my dick has taken a liking to Sophia St. James.

Once back inside, I unbutton the white, no longer starched button down and shrug it off. It falls into a soaked pile on the floor. There are some battery-operated lamps that we've turned on throughout the suite, but the generator hasn't kicked on. Fuck, my shoulder is aching. Must be the storm.

"You'd think that before our best friends decided to leave us stranded, parent-trapped on a yacht in the middle of the Atlantic, they'd check the freaking weather!" Sophia screeches, pacing back and forth on the plush carpet. She's obviously frazzled and, even in her drunken state, uptight and anxious.

"Sophia," I walk over until I'm directly in front of her and place my hands on her arms to stop her pacing. "You're going to wear a hole in the carpet. Everything is fine. It's just a storm, and it'll pass, and you'll still be able to hate me tomorrow."

That makes her grin, her plump lips lifting at the corner while she tries to tamp the smile back down.

"For now, there's still an entire bottle of tequila that has our names on it. I, Hayes Davis, am challenging *THE* Sophia St. James to a tequila competition. Loser has to go outside and check on the generator."

Her eyes widen, and a shudder passes through her body. "I am *not* going up there, Davis."

I shrug, "Well, better sit your hot little ass right there and grab a lime, because I'm gonna drink you under this table."

She giggles, then skips over to the chair and sits down, slapping her hands on the table.

"You asked for it."

An hour later, we are both completely shit-faced drunk.

"Another!" she demands, tossing back the clear liquid without even making a face and slamming the shot glass down on the table.

"Fuck, you win," I lie, pushing away the last shot. First of all, I don't trust her drunk ass not to go overboard on the deck even without a storm like this raging on, and I do not feel like going in after her.

Secondly, I've had enough tequila to last a lifetime. My eyes go to the now-empty bottle, and I realize how much of a fucking hangover we're both going to have tomorrow. The last thing I want to do is clean up puke tonight.

"Told you I'd win. You're the loser! Up and at 'em." She ambles over to where I'm sitting and tugs on my arm, trying to pull me up from the chair. It's comical, seeing as how I have a good foot and some inches on her.

A particularly large wave hits, causing the boat to lurch and Sophia to stumble, pulling me with her. Thankfully, I've got the grace of a fucking ballerina and my hands catch the floor. Sophia's now panting chest touches my own bare chest, my body hovering over hers. I can feel the heat from her body and the pants of her breath against my lips. Another inch, and I can close the distance, taking her sweet fucking lips like I've been dying to all night.

I wait for a sign, a signal, anything from her showing that she wants this as bad as I do, and when her lips swivel against me, I give in.

"Fuck it."

I slam my lips onto hers and taste her mouth, the tequila bitter on her lips as I slip my tongue into her mouth and suck the sweetness on her tongue. Sophia's hands fist my sides, and I drop down further, pressing every hard plane of myself into her. I break free to drop my head to her neck, sucking, biting, and tasting the salty skin there.

"Hayes," she moans, her voice breathy and full of lust. Our kisses become a fumbled, teeth clanking together, noses bumping frenzy that can only be a result of the pent-up aggression and tension that have finally broken free.

When her hand slips into the waistband of my pants and she wraps her small fist around me, it's over.

We'll deal with the fall out tomorrow, but tonight…tonight, Sophia St. James is mine.

CHAPTER SEVEN

Sophia

I may be having the best dream of my life. It seems so real—I can practically feel the sun kissing my skin in the most delicious way, wrapping around me like a warm, sweaty blanket.

Wait, sweaty?

My eyes pop open when I realize it's not a dream. The sun is so bright I have to squint with one eye to even hold them open.

Oh god, my head. It hurts. Pain shoots from one side to the other as I struggle to lift myself from the cloud of cotton I'm sleeping on. A snore sounds from behind me, and I scream, scrambling from the bed and pulling the sheet with me, struggling to get the satin around me since I'm as naked as the day I was born.

Surprisingly, my nakedness is the last thing on my mind when I spot a very, very naked Hayes in the bed I just scrambled from. His hair is sticking up in twelve different directions, and he looks at me through one small, squinted eye. He's ridiculously handsome, even with bed hair and—I'm sure—morning breath, and I can't help that my eyes drift down his chest to the smattering of hair there that goes lower and lower and...

Oh god. Hayes, naked, in the same bed with me...*naked*.

Suddenly, I remember bits of last night like a bad dream. A vivid, *very* bad dream.

There's no way that I had sex with Hayes. No way.

I would never. I hate him. He hates me. It's just what we do.

"Do you mind?" he asks, nodding towards the sheet I'm clutching to my body.

"No, oh god no!" I cry, holding onto the sheet like it's going to somehow erase the memory of my naked body from his mind. "Please, *please* tell me we did not...that I didn't actually..."

"What? Have the best sex of your life?" he says, a wide grin gracing his lips. His perfect white teeth gleam back at me, and his attractiveness only makes me more flustered.

"No, that's impossible. No, absolutely not. No," I repeat, shaking my head vehemently.

"Very possible, St. James. I'm pretty sure I fucked you on every surface of this yacht, and that's not counting the places that you fucked me...." His grin makes me want to slap it right off his smug, arrogant face.

I'm going to throw up. Right here. I did not...sleep with this douchebag. The biggest playboy in the entire NHL. Probably the biggest womanizer in the entire state. My number one enemy. I'd literally rather have sex with a cactus then come within five feet of his...

I groan.

"Don't look so upset, I'm sure you came more times than you ever have. Although, it's hazy for me too."

That's it.

I reach behind me and chuck the first thing my fingers touch at him. The small vase barely misses his head, and he laughs—a deep, belly laugh that does things inside my chest that it shouldn't. Absentmindedly, I shuffle from one foot to the other, and my heart stops in my chest. I feel the undeniable ache between my thighs and the stickiness that can only come from a night of lots of sex.

I had sex with Hayes Davis, and there's evidence between my thighs. *Jesus, Sophia, how careless could you be?*

"Hayes..." I whisper, suddenly more worried than pissed that I made this colossal mistake.

His eyes meet mine, and a concerned look replaces the teasing one that was there only seconds before.

"What?"

"Did you use a condom?"

An unreadable look crosses his face, then his eyes widen.

"Goddamnit," he says. "Sophia, I'm sorry...I don't think so, but I don't really remember much after..."

I hold my hand up, stopping him. "Are you clean?"

He scoffs, "Of course I'm fucking clean. Do you really think I'd be out here having sex with countless women without a condom?" He runs his hand through his already disheveled hair exasperatedly.

Of course that's what I think! He's America's fucking sweetheart. Everyone loves him. Women throw themselves at his feet, and he works his way through each one of them.

"That's exactly what I think, Hayes."

"You're ridiculous. Stop believing everything that you read, Sophia. I will give you a copy of my latest test results. I have never not used a condom. You'd be the first."

My stomach turns at the thought of him with another woman after what we've just done.

"Are you on the pill?" he asks, his eyes searching mine.

Oh god.

I drop my head into my hands, careful not to let the sheet drop free. I walk over to the bed and sit as far from him as I can without falling off the bed.

"No."

There's a sharp intake of breath, like he wasn't expecting that to be my answer, but I won't lie.

"Birth control makes me fat. And crazy. And gives me uncontrollable periods. Plus, I just got cheated on by an asshole with a small dick and have sworn off all men, so I haven't exactly needed it."

"Wait, he cheated on you?"

I look up from my hands and see his brow furrowed in confusion.

"Can we not talk about this? We have bigger things to worry about."

He looks away, clenching his jaw, to the huge window of the yacht, which offers a sunny view of the sea. The waves are calm and nothing like the storm that blew through last night. Literally and figuratively.

"Maybe...maybe since it was only once, we will be okay. I don't think I'm ovulating."

"Fuck, my head's pounding," he groans, still squinting in the bright stream of sunlight. "I hardly remember falling asleep last night."

I shake my head, rubbing my fingers across my aching forehead and willing myself to remember something, anything from my romp in the sheets with *THE* Hayes Davis.

"The last things I remember are the tequila shots at the table and falling onto the floor when a wave hit."

"With how sore my shoulder is, I think it must've been more than once, St. James."

I whip my head towards him and tighten the sheet around my torso, suddenly feeling more exposed than ever under his gaze.

"What do you mean?"

He stands, grabbing his boxers—which somehow ended up on top of the lamp—and putting them on, but not before my eyes get their fill of his strong, muscular body that should not look so good. It's a sin to look so good and be this much of an egotistical dickhead. An egotistical dickhead that I slept with, apparently more than once. He walks over to the fridge and grabs water for us both. I don't let my eyes drift to his stomach and that thin line of hair that disappears behind the band of his tight black boxer briefs.

Stop, Sophia. That's what got you into this mess in the first place.

"My shoulder's fucked. I've got a torn rotator cuff, and it's sore as fuck this morning, meaning I must have lifted stuff last night… meaning…"

I wince, scared of the next thing that will leave his mouth.

"You. I vaguely remember my head between your legs," he pauses, shaking his head then scratching it, "You on top of me, maybe? Maybe that was just a dream." He smirks.

"Stop," I screech, dropping my head into my hands once more. God, I am such an idiot. A naive, silly, stupid girl.

"Sorry." He walks over to the table, where the completely empty bottle of tequila sits. "Seems like we both drank way too much."

"We have to talk about this, Hayes. We had sex without protection. I know you wouldn't have to raise a baby, but I would."

"What's that supposed to mean? You think I wouldn't take care of my child?"

His face morphs into anger, and I feel guilty for saying that, even if I think it would be the truth.

"No, I just…God, maybe you at least…pulled out?"

My cheeks heat. I'm so embarrassed to be having this conversation after the fact. This should have been discussed prior to all of the antics around this stupid yacht, but both of us were completely past the point of making any sound, reasonable decisions.

"I'm sorry, Sophia. I can't remember. My brain is just as hazy as yours right now. I feel like an asshole, but we were both caught up in the moment."

My stomach gurgles and bottoms out, the contents lurching to my throat. I run to the bathroom and fall over the toilet just in time to empty the contents—mostly tequila—into the basin. As I retch, I feel Hayes' fingers lace in my hair, pulling it off my neck and rubbing soothingly along my back.

Jesus, this is the worst day of my life. By far.

"You don't have to do that," I sniffle, rubbing the back of my hand along my nose.

"I know."

I lean back and sit against the wall, letting my head rest there while I squeeze my eyes shut.

"Look, if it makes you feel any better, we can get a Plan B pill. And if push comes to shove, I'll pay for an abortion."

My eyes fly open and meet his.

"Don't you dare say that. If I'm pregnant from a night of carelessness with the world's biggest man-whore, then I'll be responsible and raise my baby. I won't need your help."

I stand and brush past him, finding my discarded clothing around the bedroom. He follows me from the bathroom.

"I wasn't being an asshole, Sophia. I'm just letting you know that if it came to that, I would support you. Whatever you need."

"How valiant of you. How about next time you have a drunken one-night stand, you think with your head, not your dick, and use protection," I spit, pulling my leggings up and discarding the sheet back onto the bed.

His eyes flit to my chest and back away when I catch him, and he expels a breath. "That's not fair. We were both shit-faced. We made a dumb decision and now, if there are consequences, we deal with them."

"Right, you deal with it all the way in Seattle, living your professional athlete life, and I'll stay here in my one-bedroom apartment and raise a child."

Once I'm finally dressed, I stalk towards him until I'm chest to chest with him. "This was a mistake. The last thing I should've ever done is let you touch me." I try not to notice how his mask slips ever so slightly with the assault of my words, "All I want to do is forget that I ever let you and move on with my life. You go back to Seattle, and I'll go back to my perfectly normal, boring life."

"You pursued me just as much, Sophia. Don't place all of the blame on me. You're just as responsible for this as I am. "

"Yeah, well, the difference is, I'll have to be responsible for my actions and, like always, you'll get to skate through with no responsibility."

I don't even wait for a response. I snatch my shoes and bag from the floor and take the stairs as fast and gracefully as I can. I've never been so angry or embarrassed in all of my life. The audacity of him.

Sitting on the deck, I don't see Hayes again until I hear a boat's engine and realize he's driving us in. I don't know how he got it started, but something tells me he could have done it last night. Why the hell wouldn't he do it then, before….the mistake. I don't look at him when he steps onto the deck, now fully clothed in his tux. I don't speak a word to the man who, like he's done so many times before, has made me feel less than what I'm worth.

From this point forward, I'm not going to think of Hayes Davis even a little bit. Not even at all.

CHAPTER EIGHT

Sophia

FIVE WEEKS LATER

A nauseating smell wafts through the house, making my stomach churn.

"Jesus, Scott. What the hell are you cooking in there?" I groan, then cover my mouth before I ruin Holly's brand new rug.

"Umm...spaghetti. Since when do you hate spaghetti?" Scott calls from the kitchen. Confusion laces his words. The aroma is enough to make me sprint from the couch into the bathroom just before I lose the contents of my stomach in the basin. I wretch and wretch until my stomach is empty and I'm exhausted.

"Soph..." Holly says my name softly as she walks into the bathroom and shuts the door behind her.

I groan and drop my head onto the arm that's braced against the toilet seat, "Don't say my name like that."

"Second time this week. It's been five weeks since...the yacht," she whispers. When I finally open my eyes, I see her holding a box that clearly reads "pregnancy test", and the thought alone sends another wave of nausea straight to my stomach, threatening to have me puking again.

"Impossible," I mutter.

Scoffing, she rolls her eyes and opens the box. "Not at all. You have unprotected sex with Hayes and, regardless of whether your hatred for him remains...you have to do it, Soph. If you are pregnant, the doctor can prescribe you medicine for the morning sickness. Hello...I've had two crotch goblins. I know this rodeo all too well."

She's right, but I'm still not ready to admit to myself that I am most probably pregnant. Pregnant with my mortal enemy's child—I could very well be growing the literal spawn of Satan right now.

That horrifying fact aside, this is not part of my life plan.

Not even close. Actually, not even in the same realm as the plan I had set for myself. Granted, my plan is a bit off course with my recent breakup and sudden career changes, but... pregnant? With an actual baby?

Couldn't be farther from what I imagined for myself.

Sure, maybe in ten years, when I'm happily married to the love of my life. Scott and Holly kind of love. Like, when she wants to kill him but refrains because he makes bomb-ass food and chases their kids around on Saturday mornings so she can sleep in.

Then, maybe a kid. Hell, even two.

"I can't Hol, I literally can't."

I pull myself off the toilet and press my back against the wall, focusing my gaze on the chandelier on the ceiling.

"It's scary, babe. I get it. But you'll feel better once you know. Not that I need you to pee on that stick to know. I already know."

I snap my head forward and look at her with wide eyes, "You do not. Stop it."

"C'mon, let's get it over with." She holds out her hand to help me off the floor. I take it, grudgingly. She's right, I should be an adult and take the test. Knowing is better than not, but deep down, I know.

The past two weeks my boobs have been sore. Everything is making me nauseous. I cried watching fucking Harry Potter.

What? Dobby is a free elf. That shit gets me every time.

I have to take the test.

I have to know if my life is going to forever be tied to Hayes, ego and all. So I can mentally prepare myself for what's to come.

Holly hands me the test, and I sit and pee on the stick before putting the top on and setting it onto the counter. Holly watches it until I finish my business and pull her away from it.

"Don't look. It's like what your mom used to say, 'a watched pot never boils.'"

"Sophia, it's a freakin' pregnancy test, not a pot of pasta. Jesus." She laughs but pulls me into a hug, clutching me to her body.

"What am I going to do if I am, Holly? I can't raise a baby." The word feels foreign on my tongue. The only kids I've ever known are hers, and I still can't tell you who the hell Baby Bum is or how to properly change a diaper. Once, Brady had a blow out, and Scott hosed him off with the water hose in the backyard.

Is this the kind of influence I'm supposed to look too?

Her arms tighten around me while I expel a long sigh, "You'll be fine. And Hayes would be a great dad."

I can't help the groan that escapes.

"I would honestly rather you shove me right off a cliff then be faced with having Hayes Davis's child."

"Well sister, you're going to have to come to an understanding with yourself about it, because..." She trails off, and I untangle myself from her arms, glancing down at the test on the counter.

A bright pink, positive sign. Clear as day. There's no mistaking the bold lines that are going to change my life.

I'm pregnant.

I can feel the panic rise in my chest, tightening, seizing. It wasn't as real when it was only a maybe. Now, it's real.

I'm having a child. A living, breathing, child that will depend on me to survive.

Black dots cloud my vision, and then...I'm falling.

I hear my name being called, but the comfort of my mind seems so much better right now. Everything is less...overwhelming. And I can pretend just a little while longer.

I groan, cracking my eyes open, and see my best friend and her husband hovering over me with concerned looks on both of their faces. Holly presses a damp rag to my forehead, and Scott's body visibly sags with relief when he sees that I've awakened.

"What happened?" I ask groggily.

"You fainted. Had Holly not been standing there, you would've cracked your head on the sink," Scott mutters.

My eyes widen. Shit.

"Sorry, Hol."

Holly shakes her head. "You scared the shit out of me."

I swallow thickly. I can't believe I fainted.

I sit up abruptly, remembering what, exactly, made me faint.

I'm...*pregnant.*

See, Hayes was already fucking my life up, and he was hundreds of miles away. What a typical thing for him to do—screw things up, and do it without even trying. Great, two people who hate each other does not exactly bode well for co-parenting.

Holly sees the moment the realization crosses my face, and she pulls me to her and whispers in my ear, "It's going to be okay. We'll make an appointment and get you in to see the doctor."

I nod.

"Somebody wanna tell me what the fuck is going on?" Scott asks. He looks so confused and I feel bad keeping him in the dark. He's as much my family as Holly is.

"Your asshole of a best friend got my best friend pregnant, Scott." Holly glares at Scott, and I can't help but laugh. Poor Scott. It isn't his fault his friend is an irresponsible dick.

"What?" he breathes, eyes wide.

"Yep." I hold up the test.

"Are you going to tell him?" Holly asks.

"Of course, I'm going to tell him. My father was never a part of my life, by choice, so I grew up not knowing what it was like to have a father. I'll still give Hayes the option to be a father if he so chooses. I won't beg for him to be a part of the baby's life, though"

"First thing's first: let's have the doctor confirm," Holly says.

"Wow," Scott says, still in shock.

You and me both, brother.

Next thing I know, my stomach lurches, and I'm running to the bathroom once more.

This is going to be a long nine months....

CHAPTER NINE

Hayes

"Good skate, Davis," Ray, my right wing, says as we skate off the ice. He offers a fist bump then skates past me towards the locker room. We were done, but I'm just getting started. I have another hour on the ice before my muscles scream at me to rest. I'm not stopping until my body gives out.

Lately, I've been pushing myself harder than ever on the ice. I could pretend it's my sudden drive to be better, do better, work harder, and skate faster. But I knew that my impromptu trip home last month had changed something in me. It had reminded me of how much I was losing.

I can't practice, I can't participate in games, all I can do is fucking skate.

I shouldn't even be on the ice right now pushing myself this hard, but I'm punishing my body for failing me.

The high I'd been chasing by partying and losing myself in

random women is no longer enough to numb what I'm was truly running from. So now I've thrown myself into the ice, losing myself in pushing my body to its limits.

That's all that mattered anymore: hockey—staying in the game that I've worked my entire life for. I spend the next hour doing drills, working on draining my body until I'm depleted and skating until my legs feel like jelly.

Only when they burn and scream at me to stop do I skate from the ice and head to the locker room to let the hot water pull out the ache. I shower quickly and throw my dirty clothes in my bag, then I head to the parking lot and get in my truck. I'm ready to get home, ice my shoulder, and fucking relax. It was a long, grueling hour.

As I'm climbing in, I hear my name being called.

"Yo, Davis!"

Looking up, I see Greer, the rookie, is about to hop into his truck.

"What's up?"

"We're heading to the bar tonight, you down?"

"Nah, man. Gonna rest up for the game. Next time, for sure. Drink one for me." I shoot him a grin, and he nods, then gets in his truck and leaves.

He probably thinks it's weird that I passed on going out, but despite what Kyle thinks, I'm going to try and stay out of "trouble" and not end up on the cover of any gossip magazines. I don't like the fact that I'm so close to irrevocably fucking up my career, and with my shoulder, all I need is one more mistake to give them a reason to trade me or, better yet, boot my ass right off the team.

I drive home in silence, reveling in the quiet, until I pull through the gate and maneuver my truck into the garage—but not before I catch a glimpse of a petite blonde sitting on my front porch in the cold.

Wait.

Is that *Sophia St. James* on my doorstep?

I haven't seen her since the night on the yacht when she tore me a new asshole and made me feel like a piece of shit.

What is she doing here? I ask myself.

I throw my truck into park, grab my bag from the passenger seat, and walk towards my front door.

"Hi," she says, not rising from her spot on the step. While it's not freezing, it sure as shit isn't a sunny day, and she's only wearing a thin jacket with a pair of beat-up Converse and jeans.

"Hi?" I say back, sitting beside her and setting my bag next to me. "Any reason you're on my doorstep in the fucking cold, St. James?"

She turns towards me, her eyes big and blue and filled with tears.

"Hey, hey, I was just joking. You can stalk me anytime you feel like it." I grin and hesitantly put my arm around her shoulders, noticing how she stiffens at my touch. "You drive all this way to talk about how handsome I am? Because you could've just sent me an email, you know."

"Shut up." She laughs softly, then sniffles. I remove my arm and look at her. She looks sad, and I hate that. Even though the last time we spoke, we said some hateful shit to each other that neither of us really meant, I didn't want to see her sad. I wanted to fuck up whoever was the reason for her tears. Not that I'd ever let her know that.

"I'm pregnant."

Two words.

Deep down, I'd known this was a possibility, but it still shakes me to my core. She wastes no time with pleasantries, cutting right to the chase. My body goes rigid, the breath rushing from my lungs in a harsh whoosh. My heart pounds in my chest like a drum, loud and so hard I feel it all the way to my feet.

"You sure?" I ask stupidly.

She scoffs, reaching into the pocket of her sweater and thrusting a bunch of sticks into my hands. A fuck ton, by the looks of it.

I've never actually seen a pregnancy test before this moment, except on the shelf of a grocery store, and never in five million fucking years did I think Sophia St. James would be shoving a bundle of them into my hands on the front step of my house.

"Pretty fucking sure Hayes." Her voice breaks, and the tears begin spilling over her eyes.

I'm in shock, I think. I look down at the tests in my hands, each one of them reading positive in bold, black, digital text. Undeniable.

I'm going to be a father. I'm having a baby with someone who hates me, wholly.

Even more now that she was to be tied to me for the next

eighteen years, I was pretty sure.

"Can we talk about this inside?" I ask. "You're shivering."

She gives me a small nod and rises to her feet. My eyes immediately go to her stomach, expecting to see a bump even though, realistically, I know that she couldn't be showing already. Not only, what...ten weeks later?

The reality of the situation has yet to truly hit me. A dad? Me?

I don't have my shit together. Hell, I eat frozen dinners and wear mismatched socks ninety percent of the time. The only thing I know is hockey, and that isn't going to help me be a father.

I pull my keys from the pocket of my sweatpants and unlock the door, disarming the alarm before shutting the door behind Sophia. I toss my bag onto the pile of shoes by the front door and lead her into the house.

Thankfully, my cleaner just left, so the place is clean. Otherwise, Sophia would be walking into a pigsty.

"Want something to drink?" I ask. "Water, not alcohol."

She nods.

I open the massive stainless steel fridge and grab two waters from the shelf, handing her one before unscrewing the cap on the other and draining it in ten seconds flat. My body needs the hydration.

"I wanted to come here to tell you in person. I didn't think it was the kind of thing I should call or text about, so I'm here," she finally says, breaking the silence.

"Have you been to the doctor...or? Sorry, I don't know how

these kinds of things go."

She shuffles nervously from one foot to the other, and I can tell it's something she does when she's uncomfortable. "Um, yeah, he confirmed the pregnancy. I had an appointment at the eight-week mark. I should be about ten weeks along."

"Have you told anyone? I can't...I mean, I have to talk to my agent and publicist."

"No, no, of course not. I mean, I told Holly but that's it. I knew that you wouldn't want it to get out."

I nod, then drag my hand down my face. Fuck, what am I doing?

"So, I've been thinking. And I think what would be best for all of us, with your life in the public eye, is if we have little contact. I mean, I won't keep the baby from you, if that's what you want, but I also don't want you to feel obligated. I mean, I can raise the baby myself. I don't need your assistance, financially, or your presence in her life."

"Her?" I ask.

"I don't know for sure, but I just kind of feel like it's a girl. Anyway, what I'm trying to say, what I came here to say, is if you want to sign away your rights, that's okay, and no one will hold it against you, Hayes. You live a very different life than I do, and I can't imagine that having a baby with someone you aren't involved with would be very easy for you."

"Sophia, stop," I bark. The sharpness in my voice causes her to jump, and I immediately feel guilty. "I'm sorry. But don't tell me I don't have to be responsible for this child. I made this baby—we made this baby. I know you hate me, and that's fine. Our relationship is rocky. I get it. But I want to be a part of this."

More tears fill her eyes, and she looks away, staring off into the living room and not meeting my gaze.

Fuck, I feel like I'm fucking this all up, and I don't know the right words to say.

"Look, it isn't the end of the world. We made a life. Even unintentionally, we made something perfect. I might not be the best father in the world, but I promise I'll try."

Her head whips back to meet mine, and she gives me a small nod.

"Why don't you stay the night here, instead of a hotel? I have plenty of space, and you'll have your own room."

She mulls over my offer. "Okay. I need to call Holly and check in. Is it okay if I go on the back porch?"

"Of course. Make yourself at home. I'm going to go put in a call to my agent, and something tells me he is going to cuss me the fuck out, so I might be a minute. The bathroom is there to the right, and there's a fridge full of food if you get hungry."

Without a word, she walks to the double glass-paned doors and through them, out of the room.

Holy fuck.

Of all the things to happen today, this is the last thing I expected.

"You what?!" Kyle yells. I hold the phone away from my ear as he lets out a string of expletives, one of them being "piece of shit", and right now, I fucking feel like it. I get it; he's mad. He's the one who has to do damage control in my life, and all of the shit that I've put him through this last year hasn't made his job any easier.

This being the icing on the cake.

"Look Kyle, she's not a puck bunny. She's a girl from back home. You know Scott's wife, Holly? Her best friend, Sophia. I went to elementary school with her, for fuck's sake."

"Hayes, what the fuck do you expect the league to say? She goes to the fucking tabloids and your career is shot. They'll drop you, zero question. They don't want the bad publicity that you come with, and they made it very fucking clear that they would be done with you if anything, and I do mean anything, else happened. Now you've gone and knocked up a slut."

"Shut the fuck up, Kyle. If you ever disrespect her that way again, I'll fire your ass, and my life will no longer be any of your concern. Understand?" I grit out, my teeth aching from grinding them together.

"I'm sorry man, but this is not good. Okay? We've had a shit storm this past year, and I've had to pull every string possible to keep you on this team and with a hockey career, so forgive me for losing my shit for a second."

I let out a ragged breath, tugging at the ends of my too-long hair.

"It's unexpected, but it's life. We both made a mistake, and now we're handling it. She wants to keep the baby, and I'm going to support her in any way that I can."

Kyle lets out a groan before another curse, "We're going to have to spin this, Hayes. I'll be there in twenty. And I'm bringing an NDA, whether you like it or not. It's my job to cover your ass, so let me do my fucking job."

Then he's gone.

I wander back into the kitchen and see Sophia outside on the phone still, and I'm thankful that she missed my conversation with Kyle. I slowly slide the door open and walk outside, tossing her a small smile when her eyes meet mine.

"Alright, Hol, I have to go. I'll talk to you later. Love you." She ends the call and turns to face me.

"My agent is on his way over. I think he almost had a heart attack, but it'll be fine. I just want to prepare you before he gets here. He's a bit...over the top."

"What are we going to do, Hayes?" She sighs and sags against the seat, still shivering from the cold.

"Well, I'm shit at anything involving babies, and I really don't know how to change a diaper, much less burp a baby or feed it, but I'm willing to learn how to do all those things. You don't have to do it alone, Sophia."

She's quiet for a moment, and I use the brief silence to drink in her appearance. She looks stressed. Her normally bright eyes are dull and deep, dark bags sit under them.

"Have you been eating? Are you sick at all?" I'm genuinely

concerned, even if she doesn't believe it.

"I've had a pretty bad case of morning sickness. That's how... that's how I knew I was pregnant. I couldn't keep anything down. Any kind of food smell in the morning makes me sick."

"Okay, glad we cleared that up so I didn't make you a five-course breakfast in the morning?" I tease.

She turns a tad green just at the mention of breakfast food.

"Wait, you can cook?"

I laugh. "Uh no, not at all...but I'm great at ordering Ubereats all by myself and grabbing a box of donuts."

Her eyes light up, "Donuts?"

"Are you craving donuts?"

"Maybe."

The back door swings open, and Kyle steps out, complete with his three-piece suit and the AirPods that never seem to leave his ears. One thing about Kyle is that he always looks prepared. For what? Who knows? But if it happens, he's ready. It's one reason I chose him to be my agent. I felt like he could handle any situation at any given time.

"Kyle, this is Sophia St. James. Sophia, this is Kyle, my agent," I introduce them.

Kyle looks back and forth between the two of us but doesn't bother to say hello.

Dick.

"Pleasure."

He pulls out his phone, typing something hastily before he

addresses us again, "We have to spin this, Sophia. Hayes is in a bad way, and I'm sure you've seen the tabloids, so I don't need to explain. A baby? With someone he has no intention of being with? The result of a one-night stand?"

She winces. Her mask slips momentarily before she sets her lips in a thin line and crosses her arms over her chest. Kyle is approaching this in the wrong fucking way, and now her hackles are raised—her mama bear ones—and fuck if that doesn't make me hard.

"If the pap gets ahold of this? His career is ruined. Is it money that you want? We can cut you a settlement and this will all go away."

Sophia stands abruptly, and the chair scrapes loudly against the wood as she goes to leave. I reach out and grab her arm gently, trying to stop her.

"Soph, wait. Give me a moment alone with Kyle, please."

I clench my jaw so hard it hurts. He's taken the shit too far and is being completely rude and fucking disrespectful. Regardless of who she is or what the situation is, this is my home.

Her eyes search mine, but after a moment she nods and pulls her arm from my grip, stalking inside.

The second the door slams shut, I walk over to Kyle until we're face to face, "Enough. Too fucking far. I get you're pissed. I get that I blindsided you, and you're trying to save face. But she is someone who is going to be a part of my life forever going forward, and you will respect her, or I swear to God you're out, Kyle. I don't give a fuck if hockey goes with it. You will respect her."

His eyes widen, his pudgy jaw opening then shutting while he tries to find the words.

"So, you like her then, huh?"

"Doesn't matter how I feel about her. She's going to be the mother of my child, and she doesn't fucking want money. She is not getting an abortion. I am having a child with this woman, Kyle. Take it or leave it. Spin it how you feel you need to, but it'll be done with her in a good light. Period. It isn't up for discussion."

This isn't just about Sophia; this is about my child. The game has changed—now my own flesh and blood is involved.

I'm fuming. My hands are clenched tightly at my sides, and I have to take a step back and suck in a deep, calming breath before I lose my shit on him. He's my agent; he's supposed to help me through shit, not add more stress to my plate.

Fuck, that's not fair. Kyle's gotten my ass out of shit that I should've never been in, and for that I thank him, but this isn't negotiable. Sophia is part of my life for the foreseeable future, and no matter where we stand, that isn't changing.

CHAPTER TEN

Sophia

Every second I'm here, I'm starting to think this was a mistake. Maybe I shouldn't have come.

Not that Hayes reacted at all like I expected him to. I don't know…I guess maybe I thought he'd throw a fit like a three-year-old? But his agent is a complete asshole, and if I'm going to be around him, in whatever aspect, I refuse to be disrespected.

It's not who I am, and I'm not changing who I am for Hayes Davis.

The second I found out there was a tiny life growing inside of me, my world changed. Right in front of my eyes there was a shift. It was no longer about me, but about the baby. Our baby.

Mine and Hayes' baby.

A baby.

The words still feel foreign on my tongue. I'm in disbelief that I'm going to be a mother, and with…Hayes. Together we're going to be parents.

My distaste for him hasn't lessened, It's only been pushed aside slightly—for her. I knew what it was like to grow up without a father, and regardless of how I feel about Hayes, he has the right to know. He has the right to show up and be a father if he so chooses, too.

And he had promptly pushed my fears down and said that he was going to be present whether I liked it or not. I respected him a little bit more in that moment.

"St. James?" Hayes calls from the back door, where he and Kyle have just walked back through. Kyle is looking slightly less perturbed, and Hayes seems a little more apprehensive that I'm going to pounce on him at any given moment.

"I'm sorry, Sophia. This situation is very stressful, and I'm sorry if I was rude. I'd like to sit and talk through this, if you'll stay?" Kyle says, nervously, I might add. I wonder what Hayes said to him.

"Sure."

He gestures towards the massive dining room table, and it's only now that I really take in Hayes' house. It's massive from the outside—absolutely what you'd expect from a pro hockey player— but inside is tastefully decorated. Something I know he didn't have a hand in. Most guys think black goes with blue, not what shade of curtains match the rug.

Hayes pulls out my chair and takes a seat next to me while Kyle sits across the table.

"So, I think I have an idea how we can turn this into something good. Hear me out."

I look at Hayes, who looks back at me, then we both look at Kyle.

"You two are going to get married."

"What?" Hayes cries.

"Absolutely not," I screech, in complete shock.

We both speak at the same time, our responses mingling together in a jumble.

Kyle holds his hand up, "Just hear me out, okay?"

This guy is certifiably nuts.

"Fake married. We'll spin it like this: Hayes goes home to his hometown, meets his elementary school sweetheart—that's you, Sophia—and you rekindle your love. We make it about the yacht, the godchildren you share, the whole nine yards. Make it the love story of a lifetime. Then, Hayes realizes what a catch he has and refuses to let you go again, so, spur of the moment—which we'll get on camera, of course—he asks you to marry him, and the rest is history. A few months down the road, we'll leak the pregnancy with some cute photos, and the rest is history. We'll keep you both completely out of the spotlight until the baby is born, and then after a while, if you choose, we can leak the split up. Amicable, for the sake of your child. Happily friends, but choosing to live apart for the well-being of everyone involved."

I bite my lip while his words sink in. This is the worst idea in the history of the world. I don't even like Hayes, let alone fake love him! It's already bad enough that I'm tied to him for the next eighteen years, and now I'll have to fake love him and fake marry him? Hell no.

"Kyle...I don't know about this," Hayes says hesitantly. I feel his eyes on me, but I refuse to meet his gaze. I can't. Not right now. This is too much. My stomach rolls, and if I don't take some calming breaths, I might puke all over this expensive ass designer table.

First impression to last a lifetime.

"Look, I know it isn't ideal. I get it. But this is my job. This is what you've hired me to do. Let me do my job. I'm here to make sure things run smoothly and your image isn't tarnished. This is the best way to do that. In my professional opinion, if you want to continue a hockey career, this is your only option, Hayes."

So, basically, not only am I pregnant with Hayes Davis's unborn child, but his entire future also rests in my hands? No pressure.

"This is too big of a decision to make in haste. Can I think about this? I need time." I stand from my chair and pace the floor for a minute, trying to get my thoughts in order as they race in my head.

"Sure, take time to think about it. But, please don't let this get out. I've brought over an NDA for you to sign. I know that's something you may want to have your lawyer look over, but this is for Hayes' safety and privacy."

"I'll sign it. I have no plans to sell him out to TMZ," I say with more bite than intended.

"Sophia..." Hayes starts, and I put my hand up to stop him.

"I'm not here to make a payday off you Hayes, and I know we don't particularly like each other, less the night that this happened,"

I gesture to my stomach, "but you are the father of my unborn child, and I'd never do anything that would hurt her...or him, in any way, and that includes hurting you. I'll sign whatever you need me to sign, but please stop thinking so lowly of me; it's hurtful."

Kyle slides the NDA across the table with a pen, and I snatch it up and sign my name before pushing it back.

"I want a week to think this over. This is a lot to rest on my shoulders, and I won't make a decision because I feel pressured."

Kyle nods, and Hayes reaches out for me.

"Sophia, I am not pressuring you in any way to do this. This is my fault; I was careless, and any consequences that come from it will remain on my shoulders, not yours. Don't make a decision based on my future."

I nod, biting the side of my lip until the skin feels raw and exposed. My nerves are shot.

"Can you show me to my room? I'm not feeling well."

"Sure. Kyle, you know the way out."

Kyle nods and rises from his chair before walking towards the door. "It was a pleasure to meet you, Sophia. I'm sorry I reacted the way that I did, and I hope you can forgive me for it. Please know that I only ever have Hayes' best interest at heart. It's my job to protect him, his privacy, and his legacy."

His eyes drop to my stomach before he tips his head in a goodbye and opens the door, disappearing through it.

Hayes doesn't speak as he leads me down a long, empty hallway. The one thing I notice about his house, as beautifully minimally decorated as it is, is that there's nothing personal. It looks like a page directly from the Pottery Barn catalogue. It's pulled together with finesse, but it's lacking comfort. There aren't pictures of his family, drawings from Gracie, nothing that truly makes his house a home.

Then, I can't help but think that if our baby comes here, it will knock over the expensive vases and decorations. Is he going to baby proof?

"You okay? You look like you've seen a ghost," he says. We come to a halt in front of the last door in the hallway, which seems to be directly across the hall from the master suite. Convenient to hear the baby cry.

"I'm...obsessively thinking of baby proofing and room placement. I'm sorry, I'm just so overwhelmed. I feel like my whole life has changed in the blink of an eye, and it's a lot to process."

He nods, understanding. I guess he's just as overwhelmed and taken by surprise by this, since I just showed up on his doorstep unannounced. I groan inwardly, regretting my decision.

"I'm sorry to just show up here. I just wanted to talk to you in person."

"Don't apologize. I'm glad you did."

He leads me into the room and turns on a tall lamp that sits on the table next to the bed. The yellow glow cascades around the room, bringing it into view. Tastefully decorated, it's inviting and comforting. And, after today's events, my body is screaming for rest.

I can't wait to take a shower and crawl between the sheets, even if it's in Hayes' house for the night.

"Shower's through there. There are towels and everything else you might need in the cabinets. I keep it stocked for when my parents come to visit, and if you need anything, I'm just across the hall." He gestures to the room adjacent to mine.

"I need to grab my bag," I tell him as I walk past him. His warm hand finds my arm, stopping me.

"I've got it. It gets icy at night; I don't want you to slip."

I'm taken back momentarily by the thoughtfulness and sincerity in his voice. This isn't what I was expecting from Hayes. Our lifelong rivalry was founded on Hayes' uncanny ability to make the people around him feel small, even if not purposefully. He's arrogant, egotistical, and a man-whore of epic proportions. But, maybe he's also thoughtful, kind, and compassionate.

He's taken me by complete surprise since I arrived, and I don't know yet what to make of it. Defending me to his agent, making sure I'm comfortable, and running surprisingly low on the egotistical, arrogant remark count.

I'm too stubborn to think of Hayes as anything other than the asshole who broke my heart in high school and thrived on embarrassing me, though.

I'm holding a grudge, so what.

"Thank you." I tell him, sitting on the edge of the bed.

A few moments later he returns, holding my overnight bag and wearing a small grin.

"Are you moving in...already?"

My eyes widen. "Already?"

"I just assumed you'd move here, so I can help with the baby. You know, I can't leave... because of the team." The playful grin is gone, replaced with a look of concern.

Did he really think I'd just uproot my life to move here and live in his house?

This is going to be much more difficult than I initially thought.

"Hayes..." I trail off, trying to find the right words to avoid hurting his feelings or causing issues this early on. Seeing the way his face falls, I decide to hold off on this conversation, "We have plenty of time to talk about this, okay? I'm not feeling well, and I need rest," I add softly.

He nods and sets the bag on the bed next to me before walking back to the door, but he turns at the last second. "I know this isn't what either of us expected, but I'm willing to do whatever it takes to be a good father. I won't let you down Sophia, I promise."

I give him a small smile before I nod.

I want to believe Hayes, and part of me does think he would be a great father, but the jaded, bruised part of me refuses to believe that he'll stick around for anything other than the bachelor lifestyle he's used to living.

Unfortunately, only time will tell just how serious Hayes is about being a father. I just hoped, for our baby's sake, that he is.

The irony of the situation isn't lost on me. I mean...just a few months ago, I was really engaged to a tiny dick who cheated on me, and now somehow, I'm about to be fake engaged to my number one enemy—and very really pregnant with a faux wedding to plan.

This would *only* happen in my life.

At least Hayes is a ten on a bad day. If I have to be fake engaged to someone, I'd rather him not have a small dick and be a three on a good day.

I sigh and flop back onto the plush bed.

Man, what have I gotten myself into now?

CHAPTER ELEVEN

Hayes

The next morning, Sophia is gone. The guest bed where she slept is neatly made up and looks undisturbed, like she had never slept in it. All that was left behind was a note that said thank you, and that she'd be in touch after she had a chance to make her decision.

A week ago, today.

I don't want to admit that I'm wound up tight as a fucking top imagining her choosing not to be a part of my life. Yeah, a baby is the last thing I ever imagined I'd get from Sophia St. James, and honestly the thought of raising a child fucking terrifies me.

I'm man enough to admit I'm scared out of my mind. But I'm not a coward. I'll be there every step of the way if she'll have me.

"If" being the operative word.

The thought that I wouldn't even get the chance to show her that I can be a great father is even more scary than being faced with a newborn and having no idea how to handle it. Sophia didn't say she's not going to allow me to be in the baby's life, but as much as she hates me, anything is possible.

"Fuck," I curse, flopping down onto my bed and wincing when I hit my shoulder. Pulling my phone from my pocket, I sit upright abruptly when I see Sophia's name on the screen as a missed call. I quickly call her back, listening to the dial tone until her sweet as fuck voice comes through the line

"Hi, Hayes." I wish I could see her face as she says my name.

"St. James, to what do I owe the pleasure?" I tease. Like I haven't been waiting by the phone like a lovesick fool for the past week.

"I'm calling to let you know I...I decided. I made a decision. Regarding...the, you know."

I laugh before responding, "You sayin' you wanna marry me?" I couldn't pass up the opportunity to fuck with her, but she'll likely have my balls for it.

She scoffs, but I can practically see her cheeks heating through the phone with that adorable blush, "Don't make me change my mind about this Hayes. It's not just ourselves that we have to think of anymore—it's also our child."

"Okay, okay, I'm sorry. I couldn't help it. So, you'll be my fake fiancé?"

"Yes. On two conditions," she says.

"I wouldn't expect anything less, St. James."

She pauses, then I hear her sigh through the phone. "If you do anything out of line, I mean anything, Hayes, I'm gone. I won't be embarrassed or made a fool of by you getting caught with puck bunnies. I will not be cheated on. Even if this is fake. I'm making sacrifices for you, and I think you can sacrifice that for me. I...It's a hard limit for me."

I remember our conversation on the boat, when she let it slip that the last jackass she was with cheated on her, and Holly told me how much it messed her up. I'm a dick, but I wouldn't ever purposefully hurt her.

"Done. I have no interest in anyone for the foreseeable future. I'm focusing on healing my shoulder, staying out of the limelight, and taking care of the baby."

"Two, we have to figure out some way to coexist, happily, for the sake of the baby."

Fuck, she's going to lose it when I suggest this, but of all the scenarios I ran through in my head, this is the best one. It keeps them both safe and me from going crazy....

"Hear me out, Sophia..." I pause, waiting for her to speak but she doesn't, surprising me. "Move to Seattle. I know, it's not exactly a five-minute ride from home, but I have a house with plenty of space for you both. And I'll get to be active and present in the pregnancy. Listen...I know you don't owe me anything and you hate me, but I want to be a good father, Sophia."

"So, I should just pack my life up and move in with you? That's crazy, Hayes."

"I didn't say it wasn't, but yes. We're having a baby together, and if I could pack up and move I would, but I have to be in Seattle for my job. Even if I have to take this year off, I would just have to come back the next year. I want to be able to support you in any way that I can."

When I talked to Scott and Holly about my plan, they said I was crazy...but that she had just recently quit her job, and it might work in my favor some.

"This is crazy," she says again, but this time...it sounds like she might just be talking herself into it.

I'm not much of a praying man, but at this moment...I pray that she decides to pick her life up and move in here, because I don't want to miss a single damn moment. It's true, what they say, that your life can change in the blink of an eye.

"What about a job?" she asks.

"You're pregnant. Your only job should be taking care of you and the baby. I mean, if you want a job, I'm sure you could find something, but it's not necessary. We can use this time to get to know each other and learn how to coparent."

"Okay."

"Really?" I ask.

"Yes. My father...he was never part of my life. I hated growing up without him. I always had questions for my mother, and I thought he didn't love me. I don't ever want my child to question that or wonder why her father isn't near."

Her.

"That was easier than I expected. Wow." I laugh.

"Don't push your luck. I'm actually starting to feel a little nauseous at the thought of having to see you twenty-four seven, so I'll talk to you soon."

"I'll take care of everything St. James, don't worry."

"That's the part that worries me."

CHAPTER TWELVE

Sophia

12 WEEKS

"Alright, I think that's everything." Scott says, closing the tailgate of his truck. He pulls tighter on the straps that are holding down the boxes from my tiny apartment.

If you would've said to me three months ago that I'd be packing up my apartment to move to Seattle, I would've told you that you were insane, and that I was never leaving my hot pink, velvet couch or the apartment that I adore.

But, if you would've told me that it would be because I was pregnant with Hayes Davis's child and moving into his mansion, I probably would've laughed until I cried, then kicked you out.

Blasphemy.

But, here I am. Packing up everything I own—including my couch, because it was non-negotiable—and moving into a mansion with the man I could hardly stand to be in the same room with. Did I particularly want to do this?

Of course not. I'd rather get a Brazilian every day for the next year than to do this. I place my hand over my non-existent bump and think of the life growing inside of me. The choices I make from this point on are for her, not for me.

And that's what happens when you sleep with the enemy. There are literally movies about this very thing, yet somehow, I still ended up here.

I groan inwardly. *I can do this.*

It's the same pep talk I've been giving myself over and over since the decision was made.

"Wow, I can't believe you're actually doing this," Holly says walking up to the truck and leaning against the side.

"Me either. I don't foresee this lasting long, so hopefully Scott doesn't give me too much shit when I call him to come pick me and all my crap up." I'm joking, but also not really. Sort of. Ultimately, I decided to move in with Hayes because he deserves the chance to be a father, and it's not exactly like I have a ton of things keeping me here in my hometown. If anything, I want out. And although not what I expected or anticipated in the least, here I am.

Holly throws her head back, laughing, "You two will be fine. You'll figure it out. Parenting is hard, and there's no handbook for it. You'll lean on each other more than you know to get through it. You're strong, Soph. You're resilient and one of the best people I know. You're going to be an amazing mother, and I think that this thing with Hayes is going to work out much better than you think."

Tears well in my eyes, and I blame it on the stupid hormones coursing through my body, but the truth is, I'm so thankful for

Holly and Scott and the makeshift family we've made over the years. They've been by my side through rough times, and as I'm embarking on the next chapter of my life, as unconventional as it may be, I'm so thankful that I have them.

She sees the tears and her face crumples, "Aww babe. No tears, okay? You got this. You're only going to be a couple of hours away, and I'll come visit as much as I can. Plus, you can always come home. And just think, once we find out what baby Davis is, we get to shop!" She squeals and pulls me into her arms in a tight, comforting hug.

"I know, I know. It's just change, you know? Like, it's such a turning point in life. I feel like I blinked and all of the sudden I'm fake engaged and very really pregnant."

"Ladies, are we ready, or are we going to cry some more? Hayes has movers meeting us at the house. Chop chop!" Scott calls out the window of his truck, where he's been patiently waiting.

"Let's go. Time to start your new life, Cinderella. Rags to riches." Holly teases.

"Yeah, but the couch is coming with me no matter where I go."

She laughs and pulls me towards the truck, "I'm sure Hayes loves hot pink. I think it'll really blend in with the rest of his house."

Even better, I think.

"Wow," Holly breathes, hopping down out of the truck. "Holy

shit. I always forget how ridiculous this house is until I'm here. And it's every bit of the Hayes Davis I know. " She laughs.

"Tell me about it. But because I have the worst luck imaginable, my room is directly across the hall from his. Like there aren't probably ten rooms in the rest of the house he could've put me in."

"I think it's cute that he's being all...protective. At least you aren't arguing like children anymore."

She smirks.

Hayes chooses that time to open the front door and walk out. Something deep in my stomach swirls at the sight of him. Probably morning sickness that turned into afternoon sickness.

Keep lying to yourself, St. James. I can practically hear his voice inside my head.

The old shirt he's wearing is cut from under the arm to his waist, revealing the muscles on his hips that cause me to shiver. In gym shorts and old tennis shoes, he looks relaxed and happy, two things that look too good on him. Maybe I can also blame the sudden, undeniable attraction to my baby daddy on hormones, because Hayes Davis has never looked this good.

Ugh, I've been here for all of five minutes, and I'm already referring to him as my "baby daddy." I mean seriously, does the guy have to look that good in just a t-shirt and gym shorts?

"Hi, Sophia." He smiles warmly, pulling me in for a completely platonic hug.

"Hi."

No sarcastic, egotistical comments?

He and Scott get busy unloading the truck, leaving Holly and me to sit in his patio furniture on the front porch and watch as they do all of the hard, manual labor.

"All we need are mimosas, virgin, of course, for the preggo, and we'd be set." Holly laughs, propping her feet up on the ottoman.

"Don't remind me. I miss wine. And it's only been like five minutes."

Piece by piece, they bring in all of the boxes and the small amount of furniture that I decided to bring with me to Seattle. It feels strange moving into a house with someone I hardly know—especially when, what I do know, I despise. Add in the fact that I only have a few of my own belongings to bring with me, and it's uncomfortable from the start. When they make it to the bright pink couch, Hayes stops, scratching his head, then strolls back over to me.

"Uh, Soph."

I grin.

"Yes, Hayes?"

He looks back and forth between me and my hot pink piece of baggage.

"You know, I have every piece of furniture that you could ever need here. And...I'm just not sure that this will really go with the um, decor."

I almost let my mask drop and break out into laughter, but I decide to let him suffer for a little while longer.

"What, you don't like it?" I feign hurt, placing my hand on my chest with a pained look in my eyes.

His eyes widen in alarm, "No, no. That's not it, I just..."

Holly breaks before I do, throwing her head back and laughing so loud it echoes off the front porch. "You are the biggest suck up. That couch stays, or she goes. Trust me. It took me two weeks of convincing, and I still couldn't get her to get rid of it."

"Nonnegotiable for me, Davis."

"Fine. But can it go in the basement?"

"Sure."

He and Scott unload the couch and disappear from view.

"How long were you going to let him go for?" Holly asks, her eyes bright with mischievousness.

"A while." I grin.

"That's it. You're officially moved into Casa Davis," Hayes says as our friends pull out of the driveway.

Which means, we're alone. We're officially roommates having a child together. The entire scenario is strange, and it's definitely going to take some getting used to, but I appreciate his effort. It showed when he allowed my ten-dollar hot pink Goodwill couch to make the move.

"So, I got this baby book on Amazon," he starts, catching my gaze.

I can't stop my jaw dropping in surprise. *Hayes* got a...book?

About babies?

"You are reading a parenting book?"

"Don't sound so surprised. I actually love to read."

Okay, I can't even picture him with a book, let alone reading it.

"Sorry," I laugh. "I'm just shocked. What did you read in this baby book?"

He stands up and walks over to the bar in the kitchen, where he grabs a thick book with an infant on the cover and holds it up for me to see.

"Babies start hearing things around eighteen weeks, in the second trimester. How cool is that? I was thinking we could get some headphones and play some Nirvana."

My eyes widen before the laugh escapes, "Nirvana, Hayes? Really?"

"What? They're a classic. *Every* kid should know Nirvana. And Pearl Jam."

"Okay, how about we start with the actual classics, like Mozart and Beethoven?"

He shrugs, "Fine with me. But, Nirvana eventually."

"Maybe when she's a teenager."

"You're pretty dead set on it being a girl, huh?"

Biting my lip, I place my hand over my stomach before I answer him, "I think so. But I could be wrong."

"I know things are still...adjusting between us, but...thank you, Sophia. For giving me a chance to be a father." The sincerity in his voice and devotion in his eyes make me misty-eyed, and this time I *know* it's the pregnancy hormones. It's hard to forgive, and forgiving him for the past—for the insecurity he placed deep within my heart—is hard. I can't forget, but I want to work to forgive him. For our child.

"She's your daughter too. You deserve the chance as much as I do, Hayes."

He nods, extending the book towards me, and I take it with a small smile.

It's like a proverbial olive branch. A truce of sorts between the two of us. After all, we're doing the most challenging thing two people can do together—raising a baby, which neither of us have any idea how to do. Now more than ever, I have to leave the past behind in order to move forward.

The next few days pass surprisingly uneventfully. I expected things between Hayes and me to be awkward and strained as we learned to coexist together, but they aren't. They're the opposite, actually.

Hayes goes out of his way to make me feel comfortable and doesn't push when he feels I need space. I'm adjusting to a new environment and a new life. Although, it doesn't help that in my first days in close proximity with Hayes, I'm horny, hormonal, and hating him even more than usual. I can't help this...attraction for him, and I'm honestly tired of him walking around looking so... delicious. It's unfair.

"Hayes," I call from the kitchen.

"Coming." He rounds the corner and strides into the room,

his hair wet and curling around his temples like he's just come fresh from the shower. I try desperately not to picture him in the shower, the water dripping down his hard, toned body, his-

"What's up, baby mama?"

His light eyes are shining with...something I can't place, yet something so familiar. Like he knows exactly what just crossed my mind.

Three days and I've already begun learning things about him that I never expected to. Like how he takes his coffee—black. That he's actually extreme about his health and what he puts into his body. My Toaster Strudel looks out of place next to his boxes of vegan, low fat food and almond milk.

Honestly, who drinks fake milk?

No wonder his abs look like they were photoshopped onto his body. Great, I'm going to end up a beached whale next to the literal Sexiest Man Alive.

I huff, blowing the bangs that have fallen free from the messy top knot on my head out of my face, "I've been trying to get this jar open for twenty minutes. Can you help?"

"Your wish is my command." He grins, turning my insides to mush.

Hayes is dangerous. For my head and my heart.

In just a few days, I've almost forgotten why I even hated him in the first place, and that wouldn't do either of us any good. I made sure to remind myself that I was simply a responsibility he had to take on, and that he would eventually realize that the baby and I were going to cramp his style.

It's easier to paint him as the villain I had always thought he was than the semi-decent person he seems to actually be. The further I push him away, the safer my heart is, and I'm prepared to protect it at any cost.

"What would you do without my strong, capable hands?"

I roll my eyes and cross my arms over my chest, wincing as I brush against my overly sensitive breasts. The past few days since moving in have been torture. I'm sore, achy, and more turned on than I've ever been in my life.

"What's wrong?"

"Nothing," I squeak, my voice coming out more of a throaty whisper than I intended.

"You're a shit liar, St. James."

He prowls closer, still clutching the jar of spicy pickles I had been desperate to open only moments before. I notice that the jar is small in his massive hands, and then my mind wanders to what he could actually do with those strong...capable hands.

I groan inwardly, pushing all thoughts of Hayes from my mind. Or at least that's what I tell myself.

The air around us shifts, and his stare turns molten. I feel it all the way to my toes, tingling, twisting, and turning the pit of my stomach, then lower until my thighs clench together to slow the ache forming there.

"I...am not."

He's so close now, I instinctively grab onto the counter behind me, gripping it for dear life. So close that when he laughs at my lie, I feel a drop of water from his freshly showered hair fall onto my cheek.

"Is there something I can help you with, Sophia?"

His hoarse, raspy voice sends a shot straight to the ache between my thighs.

God, I am so screwed. How am I supposed to resist this man with the amount of hormones I have coursing through my body?

He has a very unfair advantage, and I'm surely going to lose this war between us.

"What are you implying, Hayes?" I ask.

He shrugs, stepping closer, putting the jar down on the counter, and gripping the countertop on each side of me. Caging me in completely. I have no escape.

"I think you need someone to take care of you."

He dips his head down, dragging his nose along the underside of my jaw, and my legs turn to jelly. I clutch the counter harder, begging my stupid body to keep me upright and not melt into a willing puddle at his feet.

This is stupid. I hated Hayes. I always have.

Then why do just a few, raspy innuendoes make me so desperate for his touch? His proximity forces me to be honest with myself.

Do I want Hayes?

Of course I do. I'm just not fool enough to admit it out loud. Hello, Sexiest Man Alive. Even my poor, hormonal body can't deny my attraction to him, regardless of whether I want to run him over or not.

"You're crazy," I whisper, my eyes searching his honey-flecked green pools of lava.

"Maybe, but I think that you want me just as much as I want you," he says, inching closer and closer until I feel his lips brush against mine.

I should stop this. I should push away both Hayes and the hazy cloud of lust that forms around my brain the second he looks at me with those eyes. But my body is a desperate wench, and I don't have the strength or willpower to deny myself any longer.

"No. We can't. This complicates things, and we can't afford any more complications, Hayes," I tell him, more firmly this time.

"Complications are good."

I feel him place a gentle, soft kiss against the sensitive side of my neck, before his teeth nip the skin, then sooth it with his tongue.

"Have I rendered you speechless? Wow, it was that easy?" he teases. Pulling back, his eyes search mine, and I see the same desire that I feel. My hands find his chest, finally letting go of the safety of the counter.

I know deep down that the moment my hands leave the counter, I'm in his territory, and all bets are off. The second my fingers touch his chest, feeling the hard, delicious muscles that strain under the simple black tee he's wearing, I decide to worry about the consequences later.

"Shut up, Davis," I command. My hands fist in the front of his shirt, yanking him all the way towards me. I'm momentarily shocked by my brazen move, but the past four days have been torture. I'm wound tight and desperate for him to ease that tightness.

I can feel him smile against my lips until my tongue darts out and licks the seam of his, Then the smile is gone, replaced with frenzy. Together, we're a mess of bumped teeth and hands that can't stop. This time, I'll remember every single second of being touched by Hayes Davis. I will savor it and relive it because this is never ever happening again.

Keep lying to yourself, St. James.

Panting, I murmur, "Wait, wait, wait," when his hands snake underneath the thin cotton of my t-shirt, moving against the soft flesh of my stomach.

"Okay."

He pulls back, his breath as erratic as mine as his eyes bore into mine.

"One time. That's it. Then we pretend it never happened. When it's over, we go back to coexisting. You on your side of the hall, me on mine."

His brow crinkles, and he opens his mouth as if he is going to say something but closes it again, clenching his jaw.

"Non-negotiable, Hayes. I'm pregnant with your child—I'm horny and hormonal, and all of this is your fault!"

He has the audacity to laugh but quickly corrects himself with a somber look.

"I'm sorry, Soph, I can't help that you find me so attractive."

I launch myself at him, all my focus on trying to reach his stupid, smug face so I can punch it, but he lifts me clear off my feet, and my legs lock around his tapered waist with the dips that make my mouth water. With our bodies pressed tightly together, I can feel his hardness digging into my most sensitive spot.

"This is crazy," I pant as he kisses a path down my neck to my chest, sucking small spots of skin into his mouth along the way and rolling them with his tongue.

"Stop thinking."

Pulling his lips from my skin, he lays me back on the cold granite, sliding his hand up and up until he reaches the lace of my bra. His fingers trail lightly over the cup until he reaches the swell of skin. The contact sends my back bowing from the counter, pushing myself closer to his touch.

"Hayes..." I moan breathlessly.

"So responsive," he murmurs. He dips his hand inside the cup of my bra to my now much larger breasts and grabs a handful, squeezing gently.

"Fuck, you're perfect, Sophia."

I bite my lip to stop the moan, but barely succeed. My body is lit up like a firework. Every brush of his hand sends shivers through me, and every time he grinds against the apex of my thighs, his hardness brushing over my clit through my thin sleep shorts, I feel like I might actually come.

Holy shit. What is he doing to me?

The second the rough pad of his thumb ghosts over my nipple,

I squeeze my thighs together instinctively. I feel the delicious snake of my orgasm wind its way up my body, warming everything down to my toes.

"Sophia?" Hayes asks, pinching my nipple lightly and rolling it between his thumb and forefinger. This time, the moan does escape. "Are you going to come, just from me playing with your nipples?"

His voice is scratchy, hoarse, and full of need, and it makes me even hotter.

"I can't help it. It's the hormones...the baby..." I breathe, trying not to think about anything but Hayes's magical fingers. Fingers that better not stop what they're doing, or I'm going to make sure he can never use said fingers ever again.

"You are the hottest fucking thing I've ever seen." He groans, then brings his hot mouth to my nipple, sucking it into his mouth.

I'm so close. I can't hold on as the orgasm takes hold of my body, and I grind myself against his hardness, my clit tingling with anticipation.

"Hayes," I moan.

Suddenly, my cotton shorts are shoved aside and Hayes finds me wet and dripping. He rubs his thumb against my clit, and I rock into his touch. When he slides a finger inside of me, I feel myself stretch around him.

"Goddamn, Sophia. You're so tight," he pants. He's as close to losing control as I am, and if we don't stop, I'm going to push him onto the floor of this kitchen and ride him until we're both spent.

Jeez, Sophia. Who are you right now?

A woman who is currently being fingerbanged by her fake fiancé/baby daddy on the floor of his ridiculously large and pristine kitchen, that's who.

I'm distracted only momentarily until Hayes sucks my nipple back into his mouth, dragging his teeth against the sensitive peak and adding another finger inside of me.

Wow, he truly is a man of so many talents. Sucks that this is only a one-time thing, but this should be enough to tide me over until I buy a ridiculously awesome vibrator, and then I'll be fine.

"I want to be inside you," he groans.

I don't answer but begin yanking the black shirt over his head, until it gets stuck and he has to help me pull it the rest of the way. Once it's off, I can fully appreciate his body. His physique is immaculate. He obviously spends time in the gym working on himself, and I admire that. Pair that with his grueling hockey practices and strength conditioning, and the man was lethal—on and off the ice. Right now, he threatened to kill me with his magical fingers.

I place my hands on his stomach, dragging my nails down until I reach the line of hair that disappears beneath the waistband of his shorts and black boxer briefs.

God he's sinful, and this is the very last thing we should be doing. It's going to complicate things, but I'm was too far gone now to stop.

"I'm not having sex with you on my kitchen counter, Soph."

I pull back, removing my hands from him. "Well, why not?"

"Because, it has to be uncomfortable. And I want to take my time and worship every inch of you."

Now I'm annoyed because he's removed his magical fingers from my body and pulled the lace cup of my bra back up, putting an end to the fun time.

"Oh, so now you're worried about being the hero? Guess what, I like the villains more anyway." I huff, hopping down from the counter.

I hate the laugh that leaves his lips because I'm one hundred percent serious and feeling rejected. Why the sudden change of heart? I pull my shirt up all the way and adjust it, avoiding his eyes.

"Sophia." He puts his hand on my chin, forcing my eyes on him. He's so close I can count the freckles that dust his nose and the flecks of gold that line his deep green irises. "If you think for one second that I don't want to fuck you so hard you feel me tonight when you're tucked into your bed across the hall, clenching your thighs together and trying to be quiet as you bring yourself over the edge like you do most nights...you're insane." His thumb swipes along my bottom lip in a rough gesture that sends a shiver down my spine. "There's nothing I want more. But I always do it wrong, Sophia. I never get shit right, and I refuse to fuck this up."

"You're right, it was a one-time thing, and it isn't happening again."

He shrugs, "If that's what you want to tell yourself, but that doesn't mean that's how it's going to go. Either way, I'll respect you because that's what's important to me: you and the baby."

I soften, slightly.

I'm still horny, wound tight, and now have the worst case of lady blue balls in history. It's official.

Hayes Davis is a clit tease.

CHAPTER THIRTEEN

Sophia

"Remind me again why we have to do this?" I ask, my brow furrowed in frustration. A headache had formed there this morning and never gone away. I rub at the spot attempting to ease some of the tension and failing miserably.

"Because we told Kyle we'll do whatever it takes to keep both of us in the good graces of social magazines. That's the whole point of our fake engagement, Soph."

Hayes is standing in front of the mirror in the hallway, smoothing his hair out of his face. He looks entirely too good in his pressed black button down and dark jeans with loafers. How a man can look this good with absolutely no effort, I will never understand.

I'm a total ball of nerves, and he is cool as a damn cucumber. I might puke from nervousness.

No, really, I might. The medicine my new doctor prescribed seems to not be doing the job right now. It doesn't help that Kyle had an entire team of stylists, makeup artists, and hairdressers in my face at seven am this morning. I've been plucked, waxed, and styled to perfection. The makeup on my face is more than I put on in a year, but it does look great. I catch a glimpse of my reflection and decide, I love my hair this way, but I honestly can't wait to get out of these jeans and back into pajama pants.

"You look amazing," Hayes says. Our eyes connect through the mirror, and I give him a shy smile.

The man is a literal model, and his compliments make me feel... weird.

I'm not used to compliments from him. What I'm used to is our constant bickering and the headache that generally comes from being in the same room as him.

I can't deny that things *have* changed between us. Well, more like something has changed in Hayes.

"Thanks."

"Ready?' he asks.

"Uh, yeah. Let me just grab my purse and go pee really quick."

That seems to be all that I do lately: pee. And pee more. Then... pee again.

It was a never-ending cycle, and I never knew it was possible to loathe an inanimate object like I currently do. The toilet could suck it.

"You okay? You look like you want to stab me right now."

He's teasing, but he's not too far off base.

"I'm already sick of having to pee every five seconds, but...

welcome to pregnancy." I laugh, then walk—albeit slowly in these ridiculous wedges—to my room to grab my purse and go to the bathroom.

When I walk back out, Hayes is leaning against the counter reading the baby book. Only now, there's at least fifty different colored tabs sticking out, and it looks like he's washed it twice. He's committed, I'll give him that.

"Did you know that at thirteen weeks, babies' teeth have formed in their gums? Even though you can't see them. That's cool as hell." He smiles, and I'm blinded for a moment.

By how damn handsome he looks.

It's annoying. He's annoying. Annoyingly cute with all of his random baby facts that he's got stored in that enormous brain of his.

He's kind, and caring, and it's cute that he's so happy about being a father. This is nothing like I expected.

"That is cool. Did you wash that book? It's about to fall apart," I say as he sets it on the counter, marking his spot before he grabs his keys and wallet.

"Nope, I just read it when I have a free moment."

Lots of free time lately, it seems.

The entire ride to the tv station, I'm mentally running through all of the different scenarios of how this can go wrong. I'm on scenario five when Hayes speaks, pulling me from the disaster I've somehow formed in my head.

"It's going to be okay, St. James. Don't worry."

"How did you know I was even worried?"

He shrugs, glancing at me, "I can see the wheels turning. Not to mention you've been staring quietly out the window the entire ride. You're never quiet."

"Not everyone can be as calm and collected as you, Hayes."

"Nothing to be nervous about. We'll answer a few questions about our engagement and be on our way."

"Fake engagement." I say, "That in itself is a recipe for disaster. I'm the world's worst liar."

"I know. Just like you lied and said you liked that shirt I wore the other day."

He looks offended, and it's actually a little cute. The big, bad Hayes Davis, the country's number one defender, set to be put in the Hockey Hall of Fame, is offended that I didn't like his shirt.

"It was mustard. The worst color in all of the color spectrum," I mutter.

"I'll have you know that my mother said it compliments my skin tone."

I shrug, "Fine. But I accidentally washed it. With bleach. And then threw it away."

He gasps just as he pulls the truck into the parking lot.

"I can't believe you did that, St. James. You don't hear me judging you for your furry bunny slippers and nightgowns."

"That's because you're too busy checking out my ass when I bend over to put them on."

He scoffs, like he can't believe I even knew that's what he was doing each time he "reached down to tie his shoe". "Whatever you say."

We walk side by side into the studio. The second we're over the threshold, a producer, young and energetic, meets us at the door.

"Hi Mr. Davis, my name is Brooke, and I'll be getting you and Miss St. James situated. We have a room off to the side stocked with water, drinks, and snacks in case you are hungry. Can I escort you this way to get fitted for a mic?" She's so energetic that her words run together, and I have a hard time even catching what she says, but then I'm led away from Hayes and put into a chair as we get set for the interview.

Thirty minutes later, I've been touched up, mic'd up, and introduced to Sarah, the newscaster who will be interviewing us.

Hayes takes his seat next to me and grabs my hand, squeezing it. Panic must be written all over my face.

He leans in and whispers against my ear, "It's okay, just breathe. It's not good for the baby for you to be this nervous."

He's right. I take a deep breath and the two newscasters join us on the stage.

"Alright you two, thanks again for coming out and offering us an exclusive interview. We appreciate you being here." Sarah, the newscaster, smiles and offers me a water, which I graciously take. "If you're ready then we are."

Hayes looks at me and nods.

My first television appearance and I might puke in front of everyone.

"And we are live in three... two... one..." The production assistant says, clicking the camera roll thing.

"Good morning Seattle, Sarah here with Seattle NBC, and today we have a very special surprise in store for you. We are here with the Seattle Wolves' beloved defender, Hayes Davis—and someone very important to him."

The camera cuts to the both of us, and we smile and wave. Hayes does it so naturally—it's nothing to him.

"Hi Sarah, thank you again for having us here." He smiles the same heart throb smile I've seen grace the covers of countless magazines. "I want to introduce you to someone who is so incredibly special to me. I've been hiding her away for far too long. Her name is Sophia St. James, and she's stolen my heart." He places his hand over the spot where his heart is and taps it.

Oh god, I'm going to vomit.

I smile, even though I know my cheeks must be flaming red, "I think it's you that's stolen mine." I say sweetly.

Fake, right?

"So, tell us everything! I hear that the two of you are actually childhood loves. Is that true?" Sarah asks.

Hayes laughs, "Yeah, you could say so. I chased her around the playground in the fifth grade and pulled her pigtails until she agreed to marry me."

He remembers that?

That's not exactly how it happened, but close enough.

"Actually, I think it may have been me that chased you, Hayes."

I say, giving him a kiss on the cheek.

"Shh, we can't let the world know that I'm a fool in love, Sophia. I have my masculine image to uphold." He squeezes my hand. "The truth is, I wasted a lot of time not loving Sophia, and now I'm making up for lost time. She is an amazing woman, and I'm lucky that she chose me. She makes me happy. She deals with my shit, and I know it's not easy. My mom always told me that when I found the girl of my dreams, it wouldn't be easy. It would be hard." He pauses and looks at me with fire in his eyes, "Love is easy. But finding a way to love each other through the hard times are the times...that's what you'll remember. Sophia is it for me. Forever."

His words strike a chord in me. The way that those lies so easily tumble from his lips... and the smallest part of me wishes that they were the truth. The same part of me knows that Hayes isn't capable of being with only one woman.

I remember it like it was yesterday. I won't give him the chance to break my heart again.

"That's so sweet, Hayes. Sophia, how are you adjusting to the professional hockey player lifestyle?"

"Well, it's been an adjustment, that's for sure. I mean, like any couple, we have our ups and downs. We aren't perfect, but the important thing at the end of the day is that we trust each other, and when things get hard, we lean on each other. The rest of it is just background noise. All we see is each other."

Sarah makes a face that says she's as in love with Hayes as I pretend to be.

The rest of the interview is quick and thankfully goes off without a hitch. Hayes has the entire world fooled that he's the doting, hopelessly in love fiancé, and I'm the lucky lady to be. Just as Kyle would have hoped.

"I love seeing this side of you, Hayes. Sophia, let's see the ring, girl!"

I extend my hand, showing her the absolutely ridiculous, most not me ring on the planet, and her jaw drops.

"Wow, he did good!" She grins and gives the camera a wink. "Well guys, thank you so much for coming today. I had a great time learning more about you, Sophia, and Hayes, I just have to say...you are one lucky man. Not only is she beautiful, but she's obviously also as crazy about you as you are about her. I wish you two a lifetime of happiness. Congratulations on your upcoming nuptials. I can't wait to see the venue that you choose!"

With that, she smiles at the camera, and the lights come on.

It's over.

I exhale. We made it.

Surprisingly, I'm less nervous than I was when I walked in, but that's because I can't stop thinking about what Hayes said.

When we're home and I finally kick off the wedges that have my feet aching, Hayes looks at me and says, "Thank you, Sophia. For doing that for me."

I nod, unsure of how to respond.

Things are...strange between us. We're caught between what's real and what's pretend. The lines are hazy, and I'm honestly not sure which is which.

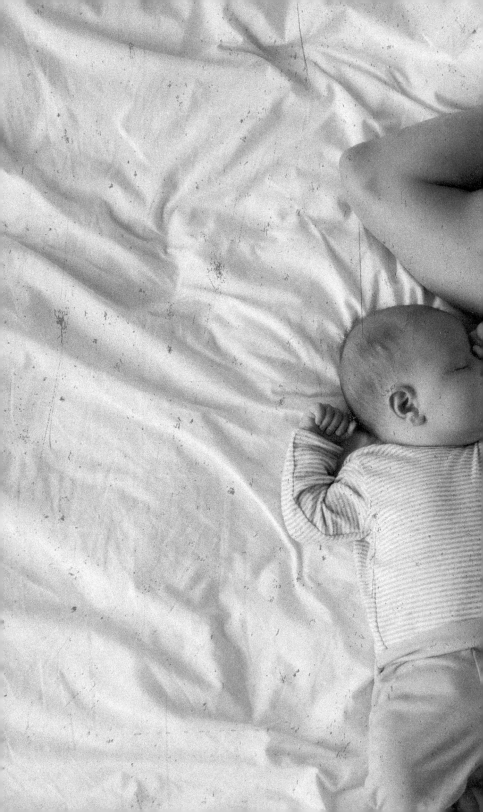

CHAPTER FOURTEEN

Hayes

14 WEEKS

I relieve stress by working out, losing myself in the weight room and lifting until my arms are sore from the exertion. That's my answer to most of life's problems: avoid them. Except my problem just happens to be my new live-in roommate who's pregnant with my baby and is a tiny, fun-sized ball of pregnant hormones. One second, she wants to throw herself at me to be ravaged, and the next, she gives me a look that tells me to stay far, far away.

I'm getting whiplash, but I've learned one thing in the past two weeks when it comes to Sophia St. James.

She wants me just as much as I want her.

And that's where my problem begins.

Since she walked through my front door, I haven't been able to get her out of my head. I can't imagine touching someone that isn't her. I want my baby mama, and I want her over and over until she's mine to touch in every way. I want every moan that leaves her mouth on my lips and on my tongue—so I can savor it.

Great, now I'm walking around with a hard on and even more tight than I was when I walked into my weight room. I groan inwardly as I adjust myself and walk towards the living room, where Sophia's sitting cross legged on the couch, baby name books spread out beside her.

We are going to the doctor today for her second appointment, and this will be the first one I've been able to attend. I'm nervous but excited and hopeful I get to see the ultrasound.

When I walk across the threshold, Sophia looks up, her deep blue eyes widening then traveling down my shirtless torso that's gleaming with sweat after my workout. She catches herself as her eyes drift past my hips, and she scowls.

"Do you ever wear a shirt?" she grumbles, chewing the end of her highlighter and tearing her gaze from me.

"Nope," I let the p pop and grin, moving to stand over her. She's got tons of names highlighted in at least five different books, and some are different colors.

"Are you...color coordinating baby names?"

Her stormy eyes meet mine and her brow furrows, "Yes Hayes. Choosing the name your child is going to have forever is a hard decision. It's one we should make after a lot of thought and deliberation. We can't just name her Sally and call it a day."

I laugh, "Okay, what about Berta? After my aunt."

I'm one hundred percent fucking with her, but the look of terror that crosses her face makes it completely worth it.

"I...uh...I mean, we can add it to the li-" she stutters.

"I'm joking, St. James. Don't worry, I won't condemn our child to a life of bullying with the name Berta."

She throws one of the books at me, which I catch with ease. I look down at the book I'm holding, and the name Leighton stands out to me from the page.

"I like this name." I show her, "Leighton."

"That's one of my favorites, too." She smiles up at me warmly, and I want to gather her in my arms and kiss her fucking breathless.

The woman is so effortlessly beautiful. Even more so now that she's carrying my child. I feel a sense of...possession. Like a caveman who wants to beat his chest and let everyone know that she's mine. That's what I feel when I'm in her presence—and fuck, even when I'm not.

I put that baby in her belly. *My* baby.

And I want her to be my girl, but I know that I have a lot of stuff to prove to Sophia before that can ever happen.

But even in the couple of short weeks that she's been here, we've fallen into a comfortable routine. One that I can't see myself ever living without again. As much as she hated me before this started, I'm shocked that she hasn't tried to murder me in my sleep. If anything, we've become friends. Friends who will be raising a child together.

"I'm going to go shower before the appointment. Need anything?" I ask.

She shakes her head, still staring intently at the name books rather than my shirtless chest, which I know is killing her. When she's frustrated, she gets this little crinkle in her nose and between her brow.

"We're running dangerously low on Toaster Strudel."

"Can't let that happen, can we? We can stop at the grocery store after your appointment and stock up on the essentials: strawberry and blueberry."

That earns me a smirk, "You know the way to my heart."

If it was that easy, then the whole winning over the mother of my child thing is going to be a piece of cake. I'll buy her all of the Toaster Strudel in the world. By the fucking truck load.

After I quickly shower and dress in a pair of slacks and a button down, I rejoin Sophia in the living room. She's wearing a long, dark dress that shows off every curve she has. Her hair is down, curled in waves down her back, but what really stops me is that she's wearing the smallest amount of makeup. On her eyes.

Fuck, she is gorgeous.

I clear my throat as I walk in, and she smiles, "Ready?"

"More than ready."

Together, we leave the house, and I open the door of my truck, helping her inside. She's so short she almost needs a boost to get in—my tires are huge snow tires and are lifted a bit.

Shit, this isn't practical for a newborn, is it?

She must see the worry written on my face because she laughs as she buckles her seatbelt, "Relax, we have plenty of time to worry about driving arrangements, okay?"

I nod and shut the door behind her, walking around to get in on my side and pulling my truck out onto the highway. We ride in comfortable silence, and thankfully her doctor isn't far from the house. It makes me feel better that, on the off chance I can't make it to an appointment, she won't have to drive far.

The doctor's office is bright, clean, and welcoming as we walk through the front door. There are posters depicting various stages of pregnancy and babies on the wall, and although I don't feel uncomfortable, I realize I am so far out of my element.

I take a seat in the waiting room chairs while Sophia checks in. Fuck, my palms are sweaty. Is this normal? To be nervous just attending a doctor's appointment?"

"You okay?" she asks, taking a seat next to me.

"Of course. Why?"

Laughing she brings her hand to my forehead and wipes away a sheen of sweat, "Well, you're clammy for one. It's okay. They're just going to do an ultrasound, make sure she-"

"Or he."

She nods, "Yes, or he...is growing right, and then she'll go over any questions that we have. It's too early to find out the gender right now, but I think we'll be able to in the next few weeks."

Her eyes light up in excitement, and it calms me. She's right, everything is going to be fine, and I'll get to see the baby.

"Miss. St. James?" A nurse pops her head out from behind the door, calling us to the back.

With Sophia leading the way, I wipe my clammy palms on the front of my slacks and follow her through the door. The nurse gives me a kind smile, and I smile back, although it probably looks strained.

I've skated in a rink surrounded by over a hundred thousand people screaming and chanting my name. I've been on the cover of countless magazines and had paparazzi scale the fence of my house for a photo. I've been to award shows where the entire world was watching on live television. And never once have I felt nervous. But now? I'm fucking sweating.

I'd never even been fazed by the idea that the entire world might see me fuck up and make a mess of my life. But now, with Sophia carrying my child and counting on me to do right, I cared. It mattered. I didn't want her faith in me to falter, and no matter what, I was going to do right by her and the baby.

"Right this way." The nurse smiles, clutching her clipboard as she directs us into a room at the end of the hallway. Once inside, she shuts the door behind us while Sophia sits on the exam table, all smiles.

At least she's not nervous.

"Okay, Mom, congratulations!" Cheery nurse smiles then glances at me. "And you must be dad?"

I nod, giving her a nervous grin.

"First time dad, if I had to guess. I can feel the nerves from here."

Shit, not only do I feel nervous, I look it. C'mon Davis, get it together.

"Yeah, just a bit nervous. Big responsibility." I laugh.

Sophia grins, "He's more nervous than I am. I told him, it's just a checkup and everything will be fine. If we're lucky, we'll get to see her."

"Ah, do you two think it's a girl? What's your preference?" she asks.

I shrug, "I just want the baby and Sophia to be healthy. That's all that matters to me." My eyes connect with Sophia, and something passes between us. My words have an impact on her, I see it in the way she visibly softens.

"What about you, Mom?" The nurse asks as she puts the blood pressure cuff around Sophia's arm, preparing to take her blood pressure.

"I don't care either. I'm still trying to wrap my head around being a mother and having a tiny human depend on me. Don't get me wrong, I am excited, but I'm still trying to let it sink in. I just want a healthy, happy baby. Girls are fun but sassy. Our godchild is the sassiest five-year-old you've ever met."

"You're right. My daughter is at the stage where she has to dress herself, and nothing matches. She'll put on a coat when it's ninety degrees outside." They laugh together, understanding something I haven't yet to experience. "Okay, let's get you finished up so Dr. Martin can come in and check on the little one."

She spends the next few minutes checking Sophia's blood pressure, temperature, and various other things, and then she walks out, leaving us alone.

"If it's a girl, can I still teach her hockey?"

Sophia throws her head back with a throaty laugh, "I wouldn't expect anything less from you, Hayes. Scott made a comment that the baby will probably skate before it can walk if you have anything to do with it."

"He's not wrong." I grin.

"I can't wait to find out. I feel like once we know the gender, it'll be so much more real."

"Feels pretty real now, St. James."

She looks down at her stomach and places a manicured hand on it. Fuck, a primal part of me awakens at the sight, and it makes me crazy—crazy for a woman I can't have, even if she's my fiancé and the mother of my child.

A knock at the door pulls me from my thoughts and my gaze from Sophia. A tall, older, balding man in a white coat walks through the door with a bright smile.

"Sophia, how are you, dear?" He extends his hand and shakes hers before turning towards me. "Hello, I'm Dr Martin, Sophia's obstetrician. I'll be here through her entire pregnancy and birth. You must be the lucky husband?"

"Fiancé," I correct him, shaking his extended hand.

I look past him to Sophia whose eyes have widened. The word "fiancé" is still new to both of us, but it's not like I'm not proud to be Sophia's fiancé, even if it is fake.

"Well, congratulations to both of you. First time dad?" he asks me as he turns the light down and gets the machine ready to look at the baby. My heart speeds up. Holy shit, this is it.

I nod. My throat feels tight as he pulls out a wand connected to a machine.

"What an amazing feeling. Most first-time parents are nervous, scared, and anxious. There's no rule book when it comes to parenting, and most of the time we're all winging it. But I know you guys will do great navigating those waters together." He smiles warmly. "Usually, a sonogram technician would be here to do this, but I wanted to chat with you two personally while we see baby for the first time."

He picks up a bottle of gel and squirts it onto the wand while Sophia pulls her shirt up, exposing her stomach. I see the soft, milky skin that I just had my hands on a few days ago. The thought rushes straight to my dick, and I push it out of my head. This is not the time to be fantasizing about Sophia.

Get your shit together, Davis.

Once he places the wand on her stomach, there's a steady whoosh. "And there is your little one." Dr. Martin points to the small little bean in the middle of the black circle on the screen. He adjusts buttons on the machine and zooms in, bringing the bean closer.

"There are the little legs. Do you see?"

Sophia covers her mouth and lets out a sob, and I rush to her side, grabbing her hand in mine and squeezing. Holy shit, this is our baby.

"It looks like an alien," I say, brow furrowed.

Sophia laughs, squeezing my hand before Dr. Martin smiles

and moves the wand around, getting a different view.

"Yes, at first the fetus does look like a small bean with arms and legs, but there is a heartbeat and if he or she cooperates, you might be able to see them move their little legs or tiny arms. Over the next few weeks, baby's facial features will develop more, and the toes and fingers will develop without the webbing."

Webbing? I swallow.

"Don't worry, Dad. It's all a part of the developmental process. There's actually an app you can download on your smart phone that shows what the baby will look like each week and notes all of the milestones it will hit. Very cool. I'll write that down so you can reference it later," He smiles and looks at Sophia, "Sophia, I am going to prescribe you a new prenatal vitamin and those nausea medicines that we discussed on the phone. Hopefully, after this first trimester, some of that morning sickness will diminish."

"Thank you, Dr. Martin. Do you know when we'll be able to find out the gender?" Sophia asks.

Dr. Martin continues to move the wand around, showing us different angles of the baby and I'm...I'm in awe. I can't believe that we made this tiny, little alien that somehow my heart already fucking loves. How is it possible to love something you barely know? That you've only ever seen once? Yet, my heart strings tug every time I see its little feet move, and pride swells in my chest all at once.

I'm turning into a sap, and I don't give a shit.

"Are you crying?" Sophia whispers, her blue eyes meeting mine.

"What? No." I wipe the lone tear that's fallen from my eyes and pretend I have something in my eye. "Just a piece of fuzz or something in my eye."

The smile that tugs at her lips fucking blinds me. "Sure, six-foot-four, more muscles than you know what to do with, and you're crying over your baby. That's adorable, Hayes."

"Adorable". like I'm a teddy bear. Goddamnit. My testosterone is crying, no...fucking *weeping* right now.

"Told you, it's just some fuzz," I grumble. My eyes drag back to the screen, where the doctor is taking measurements.

"Okay, all done here guys. Everything is looking great, and baby looks to be around fourteen weeks. I'll see you for a follow up appointment sometime after eighteen weeks, and we can determine the sex of the little one then. Do either of you have any questions for me?"

I'm still in shock that there's was an actual baby inside of Sophia. But there is one question I'm dying to know the answer to.

"Is Sophia okay to, you know...do normal activities? Yoga, running, sex..." I trail off. Fuck, I can't believe I asked him that.

Sophia's gaze snaps to mine, and she scowls.

What? It's part of the reason I pulled away from her the other day. I was scared I was going to hurt the baby...you know...

"I'm just...I'm worried I'll hurt the baby. With my dick." I mutter.

Both Sophia and Dr. Martin burst out laughing, and then I feel even more stupid for asking.

"It is perfectly normal to have questions regarding sex during pregnancy. But it is completely okay, there aren't any concerns. Actually, sex during pregnancy is great. It's a form of exercise, and orgasm releases oxytocin, which is great for relieving pain and stress. Not to mention, it keeps mom feeling great. During pregnancy, a lot of women experience an increase in libido and have healthy sexual appetites. So, to answer your question, sex is great during pregnancy, and you shouldn't worry."

Thank fuck. I've been trying my best to keep my hands to myself, and the way that Sophia has been feeling, I'm not sure if I'm going to be able to much longer.

"As the pregnancy comes to an end and you approach birth, sex actually can help induce labor."

My eyes widen.

"Not prematurely, but the body is a magical thing, and once it's time to give birth, it can help with speeding the process along."

"Thank you, Dr. Martin. I appreciate you," Sophia tells him.

He shakes both of our hands, gives Sophia the pictures he printed of the sonogram, and leaves.

The second he leaves, Sophia looks at me like she's ready to bite my head off...gently, that is.

"I'm sorry, St. James. I've been worried about it. I had a fucking nightmare the other night, and I can't stop thinking about it."

She uses the paper towels Dr. Martin provided to remove the rest of the clear gel from her stomach and steps down from the exam table.

"You could've just asked me Hayes," she says softly. "Not that it'll happen anyway. I told you...we're coparenting, and coexisting. No sex involved.

"Whatever helps you sleep at night, St. James."

CHAPTER FIFTEEN
Sophia

You know that feeling when you have somewhere important to be, and you've spent all day working on your hair, makeup, and finding the perfect outfit? Then you try said outfit on, and suddenly, you hate life and decide you're not going because you look like a huge, fat cow?

That's me, currently.

"I can't go." I huff, tossing yet another skin tight garment onto the bed.

Hayes stands in the doorway, glancing from the pile of tossed aside dresses back to me. He looks ridiculously handsome and put together in his tux and matching bowtie. I, on the other hand, look like I ate everything in the house. Twice.

"Nothing fits. Everything makes me look fat."

I'm officially at the stage of pregnancy where things no longer fit, and my bump is becoming prominent.

Hayes shakes his head and steps into the room, "St. James, you are hot as fuck. Don't you talk about yourself that way."

His words warm my insides but do nothing to make me feel any less like a whale. There's no way he and I are appearing for the first time as a couple, let alone speaking to anyone about our upcoming fake nuptials.

Being Hayes' fake fiancé is one thing, but being in the public eye comes with a tremendous amount of pressure. There's an expectation of perfection, and if you don't meet that expectation, they rip apart every single flaw you have. I see it every day in the gossip magazines.

"How about this? You go, and I'll stay here and make sure no one breaks in." I flop onto the bed and fall back into the pile of dresses.

I hear him laugh, and then he's hovering over me, putting his massive, magical hands on each side of my head while he peers into my eyes.

"How about no. You wear the last one that you tried on, and I'll take you for the biggest piece of cheesecake I can find in Seattle."

Tempting.

But, no.

"Are you really trying to bribe me with food right now, you big oaf?! I'm complaining that nothing fits and I weigh more than you do. Food is not the answer in this situation."

He laughs and dips his head closer until I feel his lips against the shell of my ear, his warm breath dancing along the skin and making me shiver, "How about I make you come on my face before we go, and then you'll be relaxed."

My eyes widen. I was not expecting Hayes to be a dirty talker. And also...he is getting way off subject.

"One time offer, remember?" I push on his shoulders gently, and he kneels between my open legs.

"Listen, your body is changing. I get it. Not all change is comfortable or welcomed. But just think: it's changing for our baby. Our beautiful baby who will be worth it. You're beautiful, and I happen to think your body is fucking perfect."

Shit, when did he turn into this guy that could make me melt with only a few words? I'm in way over my head.

"That was sweet. Thank you," I mutter. "It's easy for you to say when you look like a model in gym clothes, Hayes."

His lips tug up into a teasing grin before he pulls me off the bed and into his arms despite my protests. "It's an hour, St. James. You are the strongest woman I know, and I mean that. You almost took me out that one time at Scott and Holly's."

"You deserved it. Still do."

"Get dressed and let me take you out. I want to show you off to the world, fake or not. Hottest baby mama in all of Seattle. It's a charity event. We'll smile for some photos, do a brief interview for the biggest magazine there, I'll shake some hands and donate some money, and you'll be home before you know it, eating Toaster Strudel, and watching *Good Girls*."

"Fine. But I need you to zip this one, because it's so tight I can't breathe."

"My pleasure."

An hour later, we're in the backseat of a limo and Hayes is sitting next to me, smirking as we pull up to the red carpet. Red carpet at a charity event.

Sigh.

I've been pep talking myself for the past thirty minutes, trying to convince myself that I sound like a spoiled brat and need to just snap out of it. This event is for charity. Plus, if the world thought I looked too fat in Dolce, then that was their problem, not mine. I'm baking a baby.

I place my hand over my stomach and take a deep, calming breath.

"You ready?" he asks. I hadn't even realized the limo had stopped moving.

"Let's do this."

He extends his hand, and I place mine in his palm. His warm, strong grip is comforting...and then I'm thrust into a world that I never thought I would experience.

The driver opens the door, and we're greeted by fans. People are screaming, snapping photos, and calling Hayes' name. He puts on the same smile I've seen grace the pages of so many gossip magazines, and it shines. This is second nature to him. I, on the other hand, am like a fish out of water. I manage a small smile as he pulls me against his body.

"Hayes, Hayes!" Someone with a large camera steps forward from the press section before we've even made it down the carpet.

"Who's the lucky lady of the night?"

My blood turns to ice. Of course the media would think I'm just another puck bunny. It's what Hayes Davis is famous for: his playboy ways and partying nature.

He feels me stiffen against him as I begin to pull away, but he holds me firmly and looks down at me, shaking his head and whispering, "Don't let it bother you, Sophia. I'm here with you. You are the most beautiful woman in this place."

I nod.

Turning towards the reporter, he smiles and guides me over to where the man stands. "Hi. This is my fiancé, Sophia St. James."

The reporter's eyebrows shoot all the way up to his hairline in surprise, "Wow, you've been holding out. How is life being engaged? Tell us everything."

"We recently gave an exclusive interview. Other than that, we prefer to keep our private lives private," Hayes says firmly.

The reporter nods, "Can I get a photo of the two of you?"

"Sure."

Hayes pulls me to him and gazes down at me just as the camera flashes. We smile, and he snaps another then scampers off to the next limo.

"Jesus, that was intense." I breathe, thankful that he's gone.

"The media is...overwhelming in general. You have to be stern and not let them think that they control your life. That's something I learned from Kyle. C'mon, let's get inside and grab a seat."

"One hour."

"One hour."

As we continue down the carpet, a woman and her date appear beside us. I'm so engrossed in not actually falling over and busting my ass in front of everyone that I don't even hear her approach.

She looks like a model: long, dark hair, piercing blue eyes, high cheekbones, and a sharp jaw. The kind of looks ordinary, boring girls like me would kill for.

"Hayes, is that you?" Her voice is velvet. How a voice can sound like sex, I have no idea, but I immediately feel like a fish out of water.

"Brielle, how are you?" Hayes gives her a kind smile, and she leans forward to place air kisses on each side of his face.

Well, great. Now I might have to fight her on the red carpet.

I can't help the feeling of jealousy that passes through me, making my skin hot and my grip on Hayes' arm tighten.

"This is my fiancé, Sophia. Sophia, this is Brielle. She's a model for..." He trails off, obviously having forgotten which company, and she laughs—a sound as fake and plastic as I've ever heard.

"So funny, Hayes. We actually did a shoot together for Dolce that time. You remember, yes?"

He nods, the smile on his lips faltering slightly. His demeanor has changed. Now he stands back, closer to me, and squeezes my hand in reassurance.

Hayes is not interested in this beautiful woman, not even a little bit, and my heart sings.

Any ounce of jealousy that I felt evaporates and is replaced by a feeling of...contentment.

"Nice to see you, Brielle. Have a great night." Hayes smiles again.

And then, in front of everyone, he dips his head down and places the smallest, most gentle kiss I've ever had on my lips, not once caring that the entire world is probably watching at this moment. Or that all of the Toaster Strudel I've been eating has gone straight to my ass. Not even when the cameras flash or a cat call comes from the crowd as he kisses me breathless. He doesn't give one shit that Brielle Big Lips is watching, or that the look on her face is absolutely rancid.

If I didn't know any better, I'd say Hayes Davis just staked his claim for the world to see.

"Thank you so much for being here tonight, Hayes, and thank you so much for being his date, Sophia. You look lovely." The foundation's chairman thanks us both before he leaves to speak with the other people in the crowd.

Now that our first event as a couple is over, I feel like I may have overreacted just a tiny bit. Everyone has been nothing but kind and welcoming, and I feel a tiny bit guilty for the way I acted at the house.

"Hayes, I'm sorry for how I acted about coming here. It was rude, and I apologize."

He looks at me with a furrowed brow, "You were upset Sophia. Never apologize for how you feel."

I'm not ready to admit it out loud, but the majority of my guilt stems from the way that I've treated Hayes for the majority of our adult lives. Even though we both said and did things that were…well, childish and immature, I have been awful to him. Now that I've gotten to know him, I see he's nothing like I imagined. If anything, he's better than anyone actually believes him to be. The gossip magazines paint the party playboy without a care in the world, but truthfully, he's kind and caring. He volunteers with youth, donates to sick children, and visits his mama every chance that he gets. Those are the things that the media should focus on, but you never see them printed. You only see the times he's caught in a situation that's more salacious.

"You're nothing like I thought," I whisper.

He says nothing for so long that I think he may not have heard me. But, it's just us in the confined space of the backseat of this limo. If I reach out, my hand would brush his on the cool leather next to my own.

Finally, he says, "You never gave me the chance. I'm not perfect Sophia. I fuck up more often than not. I make mistakes, just like everyone else. I'm guilty of a lot of things, including spending time with women I had no business with. I'm a guy. Not that it excuses it, but I just want you to know that, even though nothing about our engagement is real, and I know you still have these reservations about who I am, I am committed. I won't embarrass you by pursuing anyone else, and I would never disrespect you in any way."

My heart tugs at his words, and I feel the tears well up in my eyes. Stupid hormones.

"I appreciate you saying that. I hope that we can be friends—forget everything from the past and only move forward. Not just for the baby, but for us?" I ask.

"Like you could get rid of me." He smiles, taking my hand and lacing his fingers with my own. The gesture is simple and not something I expected from him.

I can't help the overload of feelings inside me that threaten to burst from the seams at any given moment. I'm...confused—confused about the things I shouldn't, and can't, be feeling for Hayes.

The last thing I need to do is accidentally fall for my fake husband to be. No matter how charming and ridiculously hot he is.

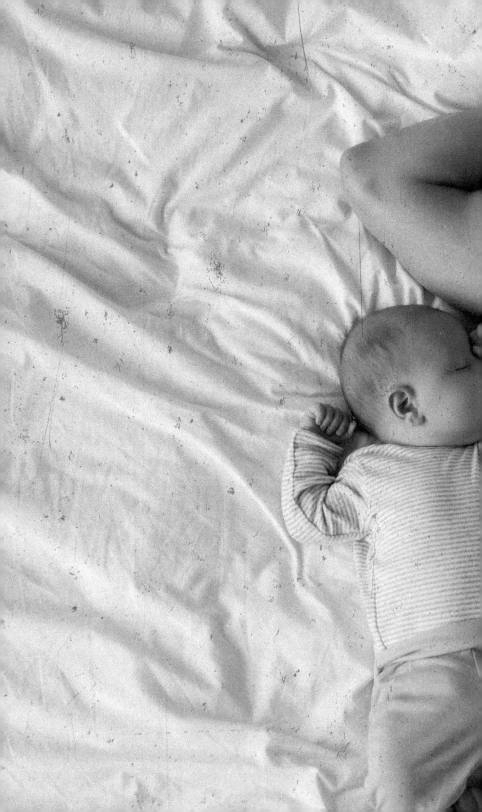

CHAPTER SIXTEEN

Hayes

18 WEEKS

Two weeks pass in what seems like the blink of an eye. Together, Sophia and I have formed a friendship. One that I didn't expect but never want to give up. That's the selfish asshole in me.

But, if I have it my way, I'm never giving either of them up.

We fall into a comfortable routine: She washes the dishes, and I put them away. I buy her Toaster Strudel, and she folds my underwear. It's a strange kind of symbiosis, but it works for us.

"Hayes!" I hear Sophia scream from the other side of the house, jostling me and making me almost drop the fifty-pound weight I'm lifting on the bench.

I quickly put the bar back on the rack and fly from the bench, making it to the other side of the house in record time. I find Sophia lying on the couch, board straight, staring at the ceiling.

"Are you okay? What's wrong? Is it the baby?" I pant, skidding to a stop by her side.

"No, I'm fine. Everything's fine. Sorry." She grins and, even though she scared the fuck out of me, I want more of the smile she's gracing me with right now.

"You scared me to death, I thought something was wrong."

"I'm fine...but I think I felt the baby move!"

My eyebrows raise, "Really? Like, on the outside?"

For the past two weeks she's been feeling the baby move at random times, and each time she's more shocked than the time before. I can't wait to feel.

"Yeah, like just a small movement but I definitely felt it."

I drop to my knees beside her, staring at her belly intently, as if my stare will cause my rookie to show herself.

Rookie.

That's what I nicknamed her when we decided we were both tired of calling her "the baby." We still didn't know the gender, but Sophia is convinced it's a girl.

So, we call her Rookie, and it fits.

"Rookie, you in there?" I tap on Sophia's stomach gently. She shakes with a giggle, but there's otherwise still no movement that I can see. I place my ear against her stomach, trying to get a laugh from Sophia. "Listen, I don't know how well you can hear me in there, but I really need you to show up and show out tonight, okay? Daddy's dying to see you."

When I'm done speaking into Sophia's stomach—knowing that Rookie can hear me but won't reply for another five-ish months or so—my gaze connects with Sophia's, and there's a wide, happy smile on her face. Fuck, I put that there.

Sophia's beautiful without a smile, but with one...she's breathtaking. Perfection if there ever was any.

"Oh, you're smooth."

I shrug, "Just doing my daddy duty."

We sit together in silence for a moment, with me still gazing at her stomach intently, and just as I'm about to get up and grab a drink from the fridge, I see the smallest movement.

"Was that it? Sophia, I saw it!" I yell.

Laughing, she nods.

"Fuck yes, I am the baby whisperer." I place my hand on her stomach again and put my lips just above the waistband of Sophia's shorts. "Thanks, Rook. I knew you were going to be Daddy's girl."

Sophia hisses when my lips dance across her sensitive skin, and her eyes have turned stormy. It's the same look she gives me each and every time she denies herself. See, living in such close quarters, I know just how much pent-up sexual frustration she holds. And each and every time I can, I chip away at her resolve, breaking her down until I can finally have her fall apart in my hands. With zero reservations and no regrets.

She clears her throat before sitting up, and adjusts the tank top strap that has fallen off her shoulder.

"Tomorrow's the day. Are you nervous again?"

A teasing smile forms on her lips, and I want to kiss it right the fuck off.

167

"Truth or a lie?"

"Truth, always."

I shrug, "Sort of. I get this weird, sweaty, panicky feeling the second I step over the threshold there. I don't know why. I guess...I don't know. I just have some irrational fears that I'm working through."

"You've never mentioned that," she says, her eyes wide.

"I know. It's not something I like to talk about. I'm a man. The fearless one."

She takes my hand and pulls me off my knees and onto the couch next to her. "Hayes, just because I'm the pregnant one, doesn't mean that you can't have any worries or fears. She's your baby too."

I nod. "I have this fear that something is going to happen to her. To you. To both of you. And being at the doctor, as irrational as it is, seems to make it worse. I've been having these nightmares, almost every night since you got here. They're fucking terrible. We're driving over a bridge, and somehow I hit a patch of ice, overcorrect and we go over the side."

I swallow thickly, pushing the fear in my throat down, "It's my fault. I'm paying more attention to some story that you're telling than to the road, and then I hit the ice and we go into the water. Fuck, it's so cold I can't even move. I get my seat belt unstuck, but I work on yours until my fingers are raw, and I can't get it. No matter how hard I pull, no matter what I try. I can't get you loose. The look on your face is enough to fucking kill me, St. James."

She turns to face me and pulls me into a hug, clutching me tightly against her body. She's so soft, so fucking perfect in my hold, that I don't want to let her go.

"Nothing is going to happen to me or the baby, Hayes," she says softly, pulling back and placing her hand against my cheek. "It's perfectly normal to have these fears. I read somewhere that lots of first-time parents are plagued with nightmares and worries of messing something up or something happening, but I truly believe that everything's going to be okay. Rookie is lucky to have you for a dad."

These powerful, deep moments with Sophia are few and far between, but when they happen, they take root in my heart and grow. Every fucking day, I'm falling farther and farther in love with a woman I can't have.

"Sorry to bring that up, I shouldn't have even told you."

"Yes, you should have. We're in this together. That's the best thing about being here with you: even if neither of us has a clue what we're doing, we can learn and navigate it together." She stops talking and puts her hand on her stomach, smiling, "And she's kicking up a storm right now. I'd like to think that's her telling you to stop worrying and enjoy this moment. Here, feel."

She grabs my hand and puts it next to hers. A few seconds later, I feel the steady tap against her stomach, and it puts a smile on my face.

Fuck, I'm a goner for the both of them.

"Now, how about dinner and a movie. The goriest, scariest

movie you can find." Her eyes light up.

Oh, did I mention, that's a new...symptom of Sophia's pregnancy? She's a born-again horror buff. Call me a pussy if you want, but after Saw VI, my stomach can't take anymore fucking contraptions. Just thinking of that shit causes my stomach to roll.

"Dinner and something...not so gory?" I say, hopefully.

Her eyes roll, "Fine. You know for a big, macho hockey player, you sure are a baby."

"Hey, don't wound me like that, woman. I'm the biggest, most macho hockey player you know."

"That's only because I haven't met the rest of the team yet."

I know she's teasing, but a pang of jealousy hits in my gut. Shit, I never thought about what would happen if Sophia ever decides to date.

God, this shit is complicated. If she ever decides to date, I'm just going to have to beat everyone the fuck up. Then word will spread, and they'll just stop coming around.

Right?

I groan inwardly. Add it to my list of "fake fiancé baby mama problems."

"My feet are killing me." Sophia groans as she flops down on the couch, the cushions swallowing her into their plush fabric.

"C'mere," I command, grabbing her by the ankle and pulling

her towards me, placing both of her feet in my lap.

She protests, but I ignore her and start rubbing my fingers along the soft skin of her arches, applying more pressure as I go.

"Oh God," she moans, as her eyes roll back in her head. Holy fuck, this took a turn.

"Good, huh?" I grin.

"Don't ruin this for me. Ah, that feels amazing."

"That's generally what they say."

I couldn't pass it up She set herself up for it.

A pillow comes sailing through the air and smacks me directly in the face.

"Ouch. Fuck, St. James. When did your aim get so good?"

"Watch it," she warns.

When I put my hands up in surrender, she all but growls that I'm no longer rubbing her feet. I can't help but laugh. So demanding.

She looks like the best version of Heaven I'll ever see laid out next me. Her cheeks are flushed, and a small smile rests on her lips from my teasing. She looks happy. Her hand is on her now noticeable bump, and it's something I could spend forever looking at.

I was never the guy who imagined that I'd settle down, start a family, and marry the girl of my dreams. That stuff seemed too far out of reach and not in the cards for me, yet every single second I spend in Sophia's presence, I yearn for it. Suddenly, all I want is Sophia and our child. Together, in my house.

I want to lose myself inside of her every night until one of us had to get up and check on the baby—and then once more when she's back in my arms.

But my dreams—all this shit that I can't stop obsessing over—are never coming true.

Sophia made that clear from the start, and it looks like she has no desire to change her mind. She's hyper focused on Rook and everything that we need to do to prepare for her arrival. Not that I blamed her. Hell, I'm so excited I can hardly stand it, and I'm enjoying every minute of being by Sophia's side for this pregnancy.

But I want more.

I want all of it to be real. I *need* it to be real. Every single part of it.

"So, my mom called today..." I say.

Her eyes snap to mine, and she eyes me warily, "Okayyyyy. And what did she say?"

Well, I won't be repeating exactly what Mama said, since she chewed my ass for over an hour, and there was a lot of screaming. I absolutely would not be sharing any of that with her.

"She says she wants to meet you soon. I told her I'd discuss it with you and see if we could go home for the weekend next week."

I can feel her tense beneath my touch. It's not something we've discussed, not with all of the other stuff we've been faced with.

How will she act in front of our families? Our best friends?

Will she carry on with our carefully constructed facade, or will she let the truth out?

The latter scared the fuck out of me. It's another reason I hate all of this—the lies, the fake bullshit we were pretending. At least, she was still pretending every day.

"If you're uncomfortable, I can put her off, Sophia." I tell her.

She immediately shakes her head, "No, no. That's not it. I'm just...I'm just nervous. That's all. What if they hate me?" She sucks her bottom lip into her mouth, chewing on it nervously.

"That's the last thing you need to worry about. My mom is going to love you."

"Does she know...about the baby?" she asks.

"No. I didn't want to tell her over the phone. I already had to tell her over the phone that I'm engaged to a woman she's never met, and let's just say she hasn't quite gotten over it yet." I laugh.

"Understandably. I'm fine with it. It'll give me a chance to spend some time with Holly too."

"Yeah, Scott's been telling me to come up for poker night, but things have been busy. Cool, I'll tell her we'll come. Thanks, St. James. But listen...." I pause, my fingers digging into the arch of her foot, "You'll have to keep your hands to yourself. I wouldn't want people to think you actually like me or something."

"Ha-Ha." She rolls her eyes, but the small smile never leaves her lips. "Wonder what would give that away. The fact that we're getting 'married,'" she air quotes, "or the fact that I'm wobbling around with your baby."

"Mmm, I love when you say that. Say it again." Instead of rubbing, my fingers tickle the bottom of her foot, which she promptly yanks from my grasp.

I prowl towards her as she scrambles backwards on the couch to escape.

"Sorry, St. James, not happening." I grab her by her ankle and pull her towards me until I'm hovering over her small frame, my head bowed only inches above hers. I can feel her pressed against me, we're so close. I press my fingers into her side gently, tickling her until she's squealing and thrashing beneath me.

"Stop, stop. Hayes, oh my god."

There's laughter in her voice, so I press my luck.

"Can't do it. Only when you say, "Hayes is the best baby daddy on the planet, and I would choose him over Toaster Strudel."

"You're going to make me pee!" she cries.

"Don't care. Lemme hear it."

I stop my assault in order to give her a chance to breathe and speak, but she seals her lips, folding them over in a zipped lip motion.

Oh, so she's feeling feisty tonight.

"Don't make me hide the Toaster Strudel."

"You wouldn't!" she gasps.

"You bet your sweet ass I would."

"Fine. Fine. Stop. Oh god."

I'm enjoying this way more than I should. I'm particularly enjoying how she's wiggling beneath me, conveniently rubbing against my cock, which is now straining against the fabric of my gym shorts. Everything about her turns me on, and I couldn't rein him in if I tried.

Yes, I'm referring to my cock in third person.

"You're the best baby daddy." She huffs. There's a look of annoyance on her face—the little space between her brows that's pinched together goes with the small scowl on her lips. The same scowl that keeps slipping, so the smile she's desperately trying to tamp down is bursting through.

"Annnnnnd."

This time she punches me in the chest. "Ugh, and I would choose you over Toaster Strudel. You're impossible, Hayes Davis."

"Thank you, Dr. Martin."

Sophia's holding the envelope with our baby's gender in her hand, and it's killing me not to know what's inside. We agreed that we'll open it together in front of our family and friends once we make it home. She said that the people we love are already missing so much of her pregnancy, so she wants to do this surrounded by everyone.

At the time, I couldn't have agreed more. But now I'm seriously second guessing our decision to wait. We have to drive over three hours with it sitting between us, begging to be opened to reveal to us if Rookie is actually a girl like Sophia thinks, or if he was going to be my mini-me.

I'm happy either way, but the wait might do me in before I even find out.

"My pleasure. Congratulations to the both of you." Dr. Martin shakes my hand with a warm smile and pats me on the back. He turns to Sophia and gives her a hug before pulling back, "Now, if you have any more morning sickness, make sure to take the medicine and try and take a few bites of crackers with a few sips of ginger ale. And, of course, call me if you need anything."

"I will. Thank you again." Sophia smiles and gives a small wave as he walks out the exam room door.

"Wow. So here it is."

She holds up the plain white sealed envelope.

"There it is."

"I want to open it so badly. I mean, we're *not*. Because we promised ourselves that we would do it with our families, but the anticipation is going to eat me alive. I am so excited!" she exclaims. Her eyes are so bright and happy. They shine with an excitement that matches my own.

"I know, I was just thinking about how I can't possibly wait another second. It feels like we've waited forever."

She nods then hops down from the exam table, grabbing her purse before turning back to face me, "Exactly, and as much as it kills me to wait, we have to. We came this far. Imagine everyone's faces. Holly said she could get this cannon that has blue or pink for us to pop in front of everyone...but we would need to give her the envelope so she can buy it. What do you think?"

"I think it would be awesome. Let's do it."

As we exit the room, Dr. Martin's nurse pops by to congratulate us and tell us goodbye, and then we're walking out of the clinic, back to the truck. Before we left the house, Sophia packed enough shit for us for six months for our three-day trip back home. The plan was to come to her appointment and, since it's early enough, hit the road and make it back to our hometown before dark.

"Great." Sophia mutters when I slide into the seat next to her and start the truck.

"What?"

"I have to pee."

"Already? It's been five minutes." I laugh.

She looks offended that I threw the "already" in there, but...we haven't even pulled onto the highway.

"And? I've got a baby dancing on my bladder. We can happily trade places, you know."

"Only teasing, St. James. Don't get your panties in a twist."

"Not wearing any."

I look over at her, my gaze immediately going to the pair of skinny jeans she's got on that are stuck to her body like a glove. Fuck, even in jeans and a pair of Chucks, she outshines any model I've ever seen.

Simply beautiful. She doesn't have to put an ounce of effort into her appearance, and she's still the most beautiful woman in the room. And the craziest part? She doesn't even realize it. She truly has no idea the effect she has on the opposite sex. It's part of what makes her so appealing.

"You wanna go there?" I ask her, waiting for a genuine answer.

Because if she says it, I'll pull this truck over and yank her into my lap right here.

"Mmm, don't know what you mean, Hayes."

"You're lucky my mom is expecting us for supper, or I'd show you exactly what I'm thinking right now."

She looks up at me through hooded eyes, "Good thing then."

The moment is broken when a car honks behind me. I curse, then back up and pull out of the parking spot and onto the highway. Finding the nearest gas station for Sophia to pee, we make a quick stop then are on the road home.

Our entire ride, Sophia turns the station a hundred times until she finds something that I have no idea what it even remotely is, and sings along. Then we stop to pee, again. After she comes out with pickles and a Sprite, we're back on the road again. An hour later, we stop to pee...*again*.

It's a miracle we make it to my parents' house before midnight. Only slightly behind schedule and with a pregnant, grumpy woman in my front seat, I couldn't wait to find the nearest bed and sleep.

"That was...." She yawns, stretching her arms over her head as we stand in my parents' driveway. The sun has just set, and the moon is high in the sky, casting a shadow of moonlight on her face. Her cheeks are pink, her eyes tired but bright, and fuck... those lips... bruised from the amount of time she's spent nervously chewing them. After that ride, I'm not waiting another second to have her.

I'd heard enough of her throaty, breathy moans the entire ride, watched the way her chest rose and fell with each tense breath she took in. I knew she felt it too—I just needed to show her. Some things can't be spoken; they have to be felt.

I step forward and pull her into my arms, capturing her lips in a kiss filled with every bit of pent-up frustration and tension that we've been dancing around for weeks. She moans against me, melting into me. The sound is so sweet to my ears, it takes everything I have not to pick her up and carry her inside.

The thing I can't help but notice? She doesn't protest once. Maybe, just fucking maybe, she's feeling the exact same thing that I have been for weeks.

Pulling back, I look into her eyes, my hands cupping her face, "Now that that's out the way. Ready?"

She doesn't speak, momentarily stunned that I kissed her like it was my right to do it. Her glassy eyes hold mine before she whispers, still clutching onto my hands holding her. "No, but something tells me, I'm going to have to be."

CHAPTER SEVENTEEN
Sophia

That kiss changes everything. It's the first time that Hayes has kissed me or touched me that wasn't in the heat of a moment. He moved purposefully and with intent, taking me by complete surprise. I didn't have time to think or protest. All I could comprehend was the feel of his lips against mine. He kissed me like I was water in a drought—like he had wanted to for so long but had held back until finally, like the opening of a dam, he collided into me with unbridled force.

Now, sitting here at his mother's dinner table, surrounded by his father, brother, and sister, all I can think about is the tingle on my lips from where he kissed me breathless.

"Here you go, baby." Hayes smiles and hands me the plate. He's being his normal overprotective self, making sure to take off the broccoli, because he knew I'd be halfway to the bathroom the second I saw it on my plate.

"So, Sophia, Hayes tells me that you two are getting married.

Have you decided on a venue yet?" Adrian, his sister, asks from the other side of the table. With her long, dark hair and thick brows, she looks so much like Hayes it's almost comical.

"Uh, no not yet. We're taking it slowly." I smile. She nods, and I go back to pushing around a piece of food on my plate.

"Sophia, could I talk with you for a moment? Alone?" Hayes' mother Darlene, interrupts.

My stomach immediately turns to knots. It means more to me than anyone knows that Hayes' family accepts me. I know we're about to shock everyone with our news, and I know that his mom was already upset about our secret engagement. I hate the fact that we are lying to everyone, but protecting the career he's worked so hard for is important. I know that he wants to tell his parents, at least, the truth, but he doesn't want to hurt them in any way. It would kill him to do so.

"Of course."

I push my chair back and put my napkin on my plate. I'm through for the night anyway. My stomach is full of too many nerves to actually enjoy anything.

I follow behind her as she leads me down the hall into a study, but not before Hayes catches my eye and winks. Inside the study, she shuts the door behind us and gestures to the couch along the wall. We sit, and she takes the spot next to me, surprising me by pulling my hands into hers.

"How far along are you?" Her tone is soft and not at all condescending. To say I'm shocked is an understatement.

"How did you know?"

"A mama knows everything, sweetheart. Hayes didn't tell me, if that's what you're worried about. He's very...protective of you. Even telling us about you," she says, "But, some things you just... know. And one thing that I know is my son is crazy about you."

My heart skips a beat, an entire thump in my chest gone with her words. Little does she know, her son and I are fooling everyone.

"I'm eighteen weeks. We found out the sex today and planned to tell everyone after dinner. We don't know the sex yet, but we have an envelope with it written inside. I'm sorry...we haven't told anyone. I wore this baggy sweater hoping that it wouldn't be noticeable until we were ready to announce the news."

The wrinkles near her eyes deepen as she smiles, a wide genuine smile that lessens my nerves and unknots some of the tangles inside of my stomach. "Darling girl, don't apologize. I'm just happy to see Hayes find someone that makes him as happy as you do. I can tell how much he loves you, just by the way that he looks at you."

What? Does Hayes...have feelings for me?

"He's wonderful. So much more than I expected. He has made this pregnancy a breeze. He's kind, attentive, and does anything and everything he can to make sure I'm comfortable and happy. I couldn't have done this without him."

She nods, "Marriage is hard work. Throw in a newborn, and it gets even harder. I remember whenever Hayes was a baby. I was a first-time mother, newly married, and had no clue about being a mother or a wife. I was learning as I went. It won't be easy, Sophia, but I have no doubt that you two will figure it out together."

Her advice is kind, and it soothes my worries. I ask myself daily if I'll be a good mother. Will I do things right? Having a child that looks up to you for everything is the biggest responsibility in the world, and I'm determined to do it the right way. I mean, I never expected this, but I'm thankful that I'm not alone and Hayes is here with me.

"Thank you, Mrs. Davis." I say. "I appreciate your kindness. I hope to be even half the mother that you are."

"I have no doubt that you'll be even better. I just wanted to have a moment alone with you and tell you that both Hayes' father and I fully support you and will be here for anything at all that the two of you need. I am so beyond thrilled to be a grandmother!" She squeals, no longer able to contain her excitement.

Her acceptance means so much to me, and now that we've had this conversation, I feel like I can spend the rest of the weekend with a lighter heart. I'm no longer worried about her being upset or them resenting us being together in any way.

"Mom?" Hayes calls from the other side of the door, before it opens and he steps into the study.

"We're just talking, son." She smiles and gestures for him to come in.

I can't keep my eyes off him as he walks closer. He's wearing a pair of jeans that show off his ridiculously perfect butt, with a polo shirt in a light gray that makes his eyes stand out even more.

Bright green and focused on me. Our eyes meet and, like a moth to a flame, I'm drawn.

"I hear that you're going to be a daddy."

Hayes turns ghostly white before he whips his head to his mother, stuttering, "I...uh,...Sophia?" His eyes plead with me to help.

"She knew. I didn't have to tell her."

"But, how?"

"Mother's intuition, Hayes," his mother says simply. No explanation needed.

Hayes walks over to where she sits and pulls her up and into a hug. Their embrace is so sweet it brings tears to my eyes.

Damn hormones.

And before I know it, I'm sobbing like a fool.

"Sophia, baby, it's okay." Hayes releases his mother and wraps his arms around my shaking frame, pulling me close. His arms are strong and unwavering.

"I don't even know why I'm crying," I sob, making Hayes throw his head back and laugh before pressing his lips to the top of my head in a gentle kiss.

His affection is too much. My emotions are overwhelmed, and I am a complete mess.

Hayes does nothing but hold me and let me wipe my snotty nose on his polo without complaint. My mind goes back to what his mom said. His arms are tight around me, as if he's afraid that if he lets go even the smallest amount, I'll fall back apart. It's a comfort I never knew I needed. And I can admit right now that I need him and his strength.

Does Hayes have feelings for me? Or is he merely doing the duty of the doting fake fiancé, and daddy to be? Do I *want* Hayes to have feelings for me?

"Dry those tears, St. James. You're too beautiful to be crying. Let's go find out what our baby is and tell our family and friends. I think Scott and Holly got here just a minute ago"

I nod but make no move to untangle myself from his hold, hoping for just a minute more of being close to him.

The truth is, somewhere along the way, I think I began to fall in love with Hayes Davis. It wasn't all at once, but rather small pieces of a complicated puzzle that had begun to fall together. I'm not sure what's happening between us, but I see him like I've never seen him before. I truly saw him.

I saw the side of him that the magazines would never portray: the man who rubs my feet because they're sore, and the same man who can kiss me breathless all in the same moment. I've been too prideful to admit my feelings for him, but after today...after the way he kissed me and the love that his mother saw in his eyes, I'm ready to admit that I want this to be real.

And pray that he feels the same.

"Get on with it you two, I have mimosas to drink!" Holly chants from her chair on the back porch.

All of our family and friends are gathered around, waiting for the two of us to make our announcement. Holly and Scott are the only ones privy to our secret, and Holly is the only one who actually knows the sex of Baby Davis. I'm thankful that she had the sense to pick up a cannon for both genders, since I couldn't get the envelope to her until tonight and I was done waiting.

"We're pregnant," Hayes says with a proud, wide smile.

A collective gasp soon turns into whoops and hollers, and everyone rushes us at once with congratulations, hugs, and well wishes.

It goes over much better than expected.

"I would congratulate you, but having to live with my brother for the rest of your life is going to suck," his brother Hart teases.

"Shut up, Hart, before I break your nose," Hayes responds.

They laugh, but I can see Hayes is serious about his threat. His shoulders are tight and his stance is defensive. *Caveman.*

His brother's only teasing.

"So, we also have another surprise. We're going to find out the sex," Hayes says, "Right now."

Holly walks over and hands us each a nondescript white cannon with an arrow showing where to twist, and we both grin and take our places back in front of everyone.

"Ready, St. James?" he asks, glancing down at me. For the second time tonight, I see something in his eyes that maybe I never noticed before. They're soft and burn into my own, and suddenly I wish we were alone instead of surrounded by a crowd.

I give him a small smile before lifting my cannon next to his and squeezing my eyes shut.

I hear Scott begin to count, "Three...two...one!"

On one, I twist and pop my eyes open as the cannon explodes, revealing bright pink confetti.

It's a girl! I knew it all along. A girl!

I squeal and jump up and down, turning towards Hayes, who's yelling and turns to pick me up and spin me around until we're both breathless.

"A girl, Soph. Can you believe it? My Rook is going to be a girl." He breathes before his lips find mine in a messy, chaotic kiss that I feel all the way to my toes. His hands entwine with my hair as he pulls me closer, breathing me in, sucking my bottom lip into his mouth. The kiss turns inappropriate quickly, and I pull back.

"God, Hayes." I'm breathless, and my voice is hoarse with need.

"Alright everyone, parties over, Sophia and I have somewhere to be," Hayes says teasingly, but starts to tug me towards the back door.

"Hayes, stop it," I laugh, "We're around your parents."

He groans and looks up at the sky like he's praying for patience, and for once...I get it. I wish we could be alone right now so I can tell him everything that threatens to burst from my chest.

We spend the rest of the evening with the people we love, and it's a night of laughter and happiness. So much happiness that my heart feels like it might explode from how much joy is inside. I'm having a baby girl, one who, if she is anything like her daddy, will be kind, persistent, and selfless. A piece of each of us in this little girl who will steal all of our hearts.

After we help his mother clean up and she shoo's us out the door, we get into Hayes' truck and head for the small bungalow he rented for the weekend. Much to his mother's dismay, he insisted we have our own space and graciously refused his old bedroom that she offered.

He argued that we were adults and needed our own space. Plus, my insomnia was getting worse and worse, and I needed to be able to move freely without worrying if I was going to wake someone up.

I call bullshit.

I think he wants me all alone so he can have his filthy way with me.

My heart speeds up at the thought.

When we pull into the driveway, Hayes grabs our bags and ushers me inside, and I'm taken aback by how quaint and cute the bungalow is. It looks like it came straight out of a home decor magazine.

"Hayes, this is so perfect."

He nods, "I saw it and thought you'd love it."

Just another thing he does—choosing things that he knows will make me happy because he knows me. He does know me, apparently better than I know me, and that speaks volumes. I don't deserve this man.

He sets the bags on the bed by the door and shuts the door tight, then turns to me.

"Sophia…" Before he can even finish, I'm launching myself at him and into his arms, where he catches me easily, lifting me until my legs wrap tightly around his waist. This time, I make the move.

Call it a moment of brazen want, or call it hormones, I don't even care. I don't give myself a chance to back out or talk myself out of it, or even a chance to think of the outcome of my actions.

I simply feel.

My lips find his, and I kiss him like I should have done so many weeks ago. I kiss him until my lips feel bruised, and his tongue dances with mine so fiercely that he swallows the air from my lungs.

"Sophia, Sophia," Hayes murmurs then pulls back to look at me. His eyes search my face, "What's the rush, St. James?"

His dimpled grin causes my heart to speed in anticipation. So handsome.

"I just...I want to be close to you."

When the words leave my mouth, he drops his forehead to mine and exhales, "I feel like I've waited fucking months to hear you say that, baby mama."

Baby mama. The stupid nickname sends flutters through my stomach, and I know it's not Rookie.

"Even though it fucking pains me, and my dick hates me right now, I can't....We have to talk."

A pained groan of protest leaves my lips, but I loosen my legs and slide down his body until my feet touch the floor. He's right, even if my out of control, hormonal AF for my baby daddy vagina doesn't get the memo.

He walks over to the bed and sits, waiting for me to take a seat next to him. I'm hesitant, because honestly...right now I can't be held responsible for my actions. We've been dancing around this for too long, and my head has finally caught up with my heart.

"C'mere, beautiful."

I kick off my shoes and walk over to the bed, then sit a good three feet from him, which makes him throw his head back and laugh...and pull me to him anyway.

"You think I'm not crazy for you, Soph?" His hand wraps around mine, and he pulls it to the straining erection in his slacks, groaning when my hand brushes against it lightly.

Oh boy. I'm in way over my head.

"I just have to do things the right way with you. I have to show you that this is serious for me. I can't imagine being inside of you without telling you how I feel. I sound like a pussy, and I don't even care. You mean too much to me, Sophia."

His eyes search mine, and his fingers brush back a lone piece of hair that's fallen into my eyes, tucking it behind my ears. Inch by inch I scoot closer until our knees are touching on the bed and I can feel the rise and fall of his chest with my own. I can see the war of restraint raging behind his eyes, and I'm shocked that I didn't realize it before now.

"I'm done pretending. You are mine, Sophia, and if any part of you, even the smallest amount feels like you aren't, then you need to walk out of that door, because I am done holding back. I'm done pretending that this isn't real and that you aren't the only thing that I want. Fuck, Soph. This is the last thing that I expected to happen, but somewhere along the way it stopped being about the fake engagement and what the tabloids would spin it out. I don't care. They can spin what they want. All I know is I want you and our baby."

I nod, "I feel the same way. I was just too afraid to admit it to myself, to admit it out loud. But after tonight, the kiss and the conversation with your mama...I'm tired of fighting it, Hayes."

"I'm glad we're on the same page, baby, because I am fucking done. From this second on, we're both done pretending."

His lips crash with mine, and even though I hate that we stopped the frenzy the second we walked through the door, it feels right to know how each of us feel. To not wonder or question what the other is thinking. Instead, I know exactly how Hayes feels about me, and that just make me want this more.

My hands shake as I fist his shirt, pulling him closer to me. My tongue tangles with his and a shiver creeps down my spine when his hand weaves into my hair and his grip is iron.

Hayes Davis is a lover like I've never known, and I haven't even felt his ridiculously large...You know what, maybe I shouldn't be even thinking about this right now.

I gulp inwardly and pull back breathlessly, "I want you. Right now."

Tired of waiting, I pull the shirt over my head and toss it to the side, my cheeks heating when his eyes pursue down my body, pausing at my stomach.

"God, you're so fucking beautiful, Sophia."

I bite my lip and look away, his gaze too much, too hot upon my skin. I stand in front of where he sits on the bed, and he brings his hand to the backs of my thighs, running them up and up until he has my ass in his hands. He bends, dropping gentle, sweet kisses to my stomach, continuing lower, until his fingers dip inside the waistband of my leggings and trace along the line of my panties.

My body is on fire. I'm humming with anticipation as his fingers dance across my skin.

I want him to hurry, to quench the ache he so easily created inside me. But he's taking his time, memorizing everything about my body. With his fingers, he catalogues every inch of my skin, from the dip of each of my hips to the marks upon my stomach from our child.

"Hayes," I breathe when his fingers finally, so gently, dip into the front of my panties and connect with my already slick center. His fingers are calloused and rough against my skin, and the feeling is incomparable—the rough texture pinging pleasure through my body in a way my own fingers never could.

"You're dripping, St. James." He sucks in a sharp breath and begins working my leggings and panties down my hips until I'm completely bare before him. I try to cover myself under his gaze, but he stops me, pulling my hands away and kissing them. "Don't ever hide from me, baby. Your body is a work of art, and I'm going to spend the next twelve hours worshipping it until you understand just how beautiful it is.

His words are gasoline on an already out of control blaze. When his rough thumb rubs a circle on my clit, my legs suddenly feel incapable of holding my weight. Lifting me easily, he lays me upon the bed and stands above me, slowly removing his clothes.

When he pulls his shirt over his head, revealing the same washboard abs that have been the star of many of my wet dreams over the last few months, my mouth waters. My thighs clench together in anticipation.

"Stop looking at me like that, or I won't last a second, Sophia," he mutters.

"Sorry," I squeak.

He hooks his fingers in the waistband of his ridiculously tight black boxer briefs and begins to drag them down his hips; my jaw drops.

My god.

"Now you're just making my ego even bigger." He grins.

I...to say Hayes is the biggest man I've ever been with is an understatement. How do I not remember this? How is it possible that I didn't feel this for a week afterwards?

My baby daddy is *packing.*

Before I even have time think about how it's even going to fit, he's crawling over me and dipping his legs between mine, and then I lose all train of thought.

"Oh god," I moan, as his mouth closes around my clit, sucking. Hard.

So hard, I see stars behind my eyes. I see a whole new universe.

Is that Pluto?

"You taste even better than I imagined," he says, before running his tongue completely up my slit, his words vibrating on my most sensitive part. The pleasure is too much. So intense—so all-consuming. He eats me like a starving man.

I can't hold on any longer, the orgasm taking me whole. My back arches from the bed, my eyes squeezing shut as more pleasure than I've ever known wracks my body. Delicious shocks of pleasure, every ounce of it wrung out by the man who sits between my legs.

He pulls back slightly and looks up at me, my desire glistening on his lips and chin; I blush furiously. It's a sight I never want to forget: Hayes Davis covered in me. It's so deliciously wicked. When he sees the color in my cheeks, he laughs, wiping his mouth with his hands and climbing over my body.

"Did that turn you on, baby mama?" he teases, and I can't help myself as I nod. I feel how hot my face gets. "Well, trust me when I say, it turns me on that my baby is inside of you. Mine, every fucking inch of you."

Primal. Carnal. Raw. The look in his eyes makes me shiver. I want it. I want more of him.

His fingers lace with mine as he slowly sinks inside of me, inch by inch, until we're joined together completely. I feel the well-groomed smattering of hair brush against my clit. He's so deep. I'm so full, and yet...I want more.

"Please, move," I plead.

A throaty groan sounds somewhere deep in the base of his

chest as I moan, "I'm trying very hard not to lose control, St. James, but fuck, you're so tight."

I stifle a giggle and inch my legs higher on his waist, pulling him in even deeper, and we both groan. Then, he fucks me.

He doesn't hold back. His thrusts are deep, each one deeper than the last, I feel him in places I've never felt, and I am addicted to the feel of Hayes buried inside of me.

Every time he slams back inside of me, I inch further up on the bed from the power of his thrusts.

Sensing I'm close, he reaches between us to rub his thumb against my clit. It doesn't take long before I'm falling.

Free falling into a state of bliss so powerful my whole body feels like it's on fire. The fire burns through my veins, scorching a part of me that will never be the same.

I'm drunk on him. I'm sated and worn out as the last aftershocks of my orgasm ring out, and his thrusts slow as he slams inside of me and pours into me, groaning with each ribbon of cum that spurts inside of me.

"Fuck, Soph," he cries, slamming into me one final time, completely spent.

He rolls to the side, gathering me into his arms, and lets out a ragged breath. Neither of us speak, both simply reveling in the comfortable silence between us, until my eyes begin to drift close. Just as I fall asleep, I swear I hear him whisper, "Never letting you go, St. James."

CHAPTER EIGHTTEEN

Hayes

❝ Hayes, I don't think that piece goes there." Sophia says softly. She's obviously worried about wounding my already frayed ego that is slowly diminishing by the second while I'm putting together this disaster of a bed.

"What?" I say rougher than intended. "I'm sorry, baby, why do you think that piece doesn't fit?"

She pulls her bottom lip into her mouth and squinches her nose as if to lessen the blow, looking so ridiculously fucking hot...She's sitting in the off-white glider that was just delivered. The same one we searched four stores for because I wanted Rook's nursery to be exactly what Sophia imagined and nothing less. Which is why I want to savor the look of her with her feet propped up on the matching ottoman, her hair in a messy bun on the top of her head, and her belly big and round, and absolutely fucking perfect. Thirty weeks already. Eight and a half months. Hard to believe nine months ago we hated each other, and now we're getting ready to welcome the biggest blessing either of us has known.

"Well, because it's labeled "three" which means that it's a finishing piece, not a base piece, per the instructions.'

"Damn instructions. They don't help if everything is in fucking Chinese." I mutter.

"Okay grumpy, I think it's time for a break. Either that or I'm going to be forced to stab you with that screw driver."

My eyes widen while her teasing grin spreads.

"Try me. Hormones are raging today."

Sighing, I set down the wrench and whatever damn piece it is I'm holding and walk over to where she's sitting in the glider, offering her my hands to help her up. I know exactly what the both of us need, and it doesn't involve fucking instructions or unbuilt furniture.

"C'mere, St. James." I pull her towards me, her belly pressed against me as I lace my hands in her hair and bring my lips to hers. Her soft moan against my mouth shoots straight to my dick, and I wonder...will it always be like this between us?

When Rook is here and things are different, will she still want me the way that I want her? Will she still be so insatiable as she has since the night we went home? Constantly wanting more, wanting me to touch her?

Her hands fist in my shirt, and I reach down and pick her up by her thighs, carrying her towards my room. Our room, since the night we went home. Sophia hasn't slept apart from me since the day that I told her I was done pretending. Soft, and pliant, every night she sleeps tucked against my side with my hand on her stomach.

Fucking perfect.

I growl, and she laughs, "Put me down! I am way too heavy for you to carry."

"Really? I'm a professional hockey player, baby, I literally plow guys three times your size out of my way. Are you trying to make me crazy? Actually, now I'm going to plow you." I say, with a teasing grin.

"Maybe." She laughs at my ridiculous "plow" joke.

"Mmm," I dip my head to her neck and take a bite, making my way down her neck until she's panting against me. "Are you feeling like a dirty girl today, baby mama?"

She doesn't answer but mews when I drag my teeth along her sensitive nipple through her thin t-shirt. Her tits have grown and I am in fucking heaven. She hates them, but I want to spend all day every day giving her all of the reasons why she's perfect, and these are God's gift from Heaven.

Fuck, I'm gonna come in my pants like a teenager.

Finally, after what feels like a lifetime, I walk us into the bedroom and kick the door shut with one foot behind me, then gently place her on the bed. She lays back wearing a grin that says she is feeling very bad tonight, and I plan to make use of every single second of it.

My hands slide up the outside of her thighs until they reach the waistband of her yoga pants, and I peel them down quickly, leaving her in nothing but a scrap of pale pink lace that makes her skin look delectable.

"You're so fucking perfect, Sophia," I whisper before dropping my head to run my nose along the lace, inhaling her scent. "Every single inch of you." I kiss along the new marks that have etched their way into her skin from pregnancy. The same marks she spends entirely too much fucking time wasted on, complaining in front of the mirror.

"These stretch marks are everywhere." She cried. Real tears. And I wanted to tell her how silly it was because she was beautiful with or without them, but she was hurting. Instead, I show her. Words are meaningless without actions.

I take my time, kissing each and every one from her inner thighs to her stomach, where she complains about them the most. "These marks? They show how brave and selfless you are, carrying our baby. You're the most beautiful woman I've ever seen. The mother of my child."

"I'm crying, *during* sex." She laughs with tears on her cheeks, but fuck it. I want her to know that I want her unlike any woman ever, and I will spend the next however long it takes until she realizes that she is the woman of my dreams. I slide my hands up her sides, against her skin under the t-shirt and lift it over her head and to the side.

Now she's laid out in front of me in nothing but her underwear, her tits heavy and full, and I want to bury my head between them and never surface. Her nipples have darkened to the rosiest of pink, and my mouth waters. I close my lips around her pert nipple, sucking, rolling it with my tongue until she fists her hands in my hair, already so close to falling over the edge.

So sensitive. So responsive. So perfect.

I reach behind my head and pull my shirt off, and hover over her as best as I can with her stomach. My lips are on hers, my tongue tangling with hers in a frenzy. We can't get enough of each other. Her hands are all over me. Scraping her nails down my stomach when I bite at her lip, running through my hair, pulling me closer to her.

Wild.

"Hayes," she breathes, pushing against my chest.

"What's wrong, baby?"

I pull back, and off of her, worried I put too much pressure on her.

She doesn't answer, but pushes me further back and onto the bed, and straddles my hips.

This is new.

"I want you like this." She moans when her pussy rubs against my cock straining in my pants. Her hips pivot back and forth as she rides me, letting my cock hit her clit over and over.

"Not without me," I growl, pulling my shorts and briefs down my hips in one motion, only lifting her slightly to get them off.

I move us further up on the bed to where she can be more comfortable with her knees on each side of my hips. Without waiting another second, I slide my hand in the front of her panties, wrapping the lace around my fist and yanking. The lace tears in one fluid movement and I toss it aside.

"Did you just rip off my panties, Hayes Davis?" Her voice is hoarse with need, and scratchy with desire.

I sit up and kiss her, slow and full of promise.

"I sure did, St. James." I thrust upwards, gently brushing against her and grin when she sucks in a sharp breath. "Did you like it, because I'm just getting started." I don't wait for her to answer, instead sucking her nipple into my mouth until her back arches.

"These nipples." I move to the other and bite the tip gently, "Are beautiful." Another scrape of my teeth. "And I love to watch you squirm on my cock, Sophia."

She moans as I bring my thumb to her clit and groan when I find her soaked, coating my fingers.

"You're so wet, so ready." I groan, pushing two fingers inside of her. She's tight and hot around my fingers, sucking me in further. I don't even need to get her ready, she's beyond ready. She reaches down and fists my cock, pumping me up and down then rubbing the head of me against her clit and I fucking swear I almost come right then.

I've never seen her take charge like this and make the first moves. She lines me up with her entrance and slowly, torturously slowly, sinks down on me. Her pussy is a tight glove as she sinks down until she's seated to the hilt. This is the deepest I've ever been in her, and I still need more.

"Oh," She moans then swivels her hips in a circle, pressing the head of my cock against her cervix.

"Fuck," I groan.

"Why haven't we done this position before?"

She lifts herself slightly and sinks back down on me, again and again. I bring my hands from her hips to her tits as she rides me. Slow, and so fucking sweet. They fit in my hands in the perfect handful, so pert and soft. I'll never need anyone the way that I need her. Never lust for anyone the way that I do her. I'm obsessed with this woman.

"I'm close," she pants, dropping her hands down to my chest for leverage as her hips pivot on my cock. Her pussy envelops me in the tightest sheath. Knowing what she needs, I bring my thumb to her clit rubbing small circles gently and watching as her mouth forms an oh, her eyes squeezed tightly shut in pleasure.

I look down and watch as my cock slides in and out of her. The best fucking sight. And then I feel the moment when she falls, the moment when she tightens on me, and the second she comes, flooding us both.

It's fucking glorious. Absolute perfection.

And she's mine.

My hands find her hips and I slam her down on my cock as the aftershock of her orgasm still pulses through her. She moans when I bottom out. Over and over I fuck her like the obsessed man that I am.

Until I feel the base of my spine tingle, the familiar feeling that has never felt so good, until I'm grabbing her hips and planting myself as deep as I can and letting go, shooting my come deep inside of her.

The primal, caveman part of me is roaring. I can't wait to get her pregnant again after Rook. Fill her with as many babies as she'll let me. If there's anything that I've realized during Sophia's pregnancy, it's that the family life I spent so long running from? Terrified of?

I was a fool. Sophia is made for me. This life we're building together will be the only thing that matters.

Sophia sighs happily, completely stated in a heap on my chest, cuddling into me, "Wow."

I laugh, my chest shaking with the movement, "That good, baby mama?" I tease her.

"Better. How come you don't do that more often?"

"Do what?"

"I don't know...get rough and not hold back."

I run my fingers through her hair, in an absentminded motion as she lays still on me.

"I'm scared to. I don't want to hurt the baby. I mean, I know what the doctor said, but he didn't say anything about being...more rough. I'm scared to hurt you or the baby."

She sits up and looks at me, still with me inside of her, "You will not hurt me Hayes. Women's bodies are made to have children. I liked that..." Her cheeks are flushed pink and I know she's embarrassed.

"Hey, stop being embarrassed to tell me what you like, baby.

I need you to always be upfront and honest with me. If you like it rougher, and like when I'm less constrained with you, then don't ever be afraid to tell me that."

She nods. Biting her bottom lip, she rolls her hips and my eyebrows shoot up.

"Again?" I ask, surprised.

She nods again.

This might be my favorite part of pregnancy so far.

"Say less, St. James," I grin then sit up, flipping us over and burying my face in her neck as she laughs.

Say less.

CHAPTER NINETEEN
Sophia

30 WEEKS

" Surprise!" Holly cries when I fling the door open, revealing my best friend with an overnight bag in hand.

"Oh my god! Hol! What the hell are you doing here?" I screech then pull her in for a hug. Well, as much of a hug as I can with a basketball for a stomach.

Her eyes mist over when she sees said basketball, and she immediately cops a feel. "You're huge Soph. God, I can't believe you're going to be a mother. Like, I can believe it, but it's surreal. We're going to have *playdates*."

I shut the door behind her once she's inside and together we walk into the living room, which looks like Baby Gap threw up all over it. There are baby clothes on every visible surface. I've started what they call "nesting", I think, and I can't stop cleaning and organizing and putting things together. I'm driving Hayes crazy, since he wants me off my feet, so I kicked him out for a few hours so I can organize in peace.

Apparently, he had a surprise of his own.

"Wow." She laughs, taking in the living room.

I shrug, "I washed everything just in case she comes early. So now I have to fold it all and put it away." I put my hand to my head, suddenly exhausted, 'There's so much to do. I still have to put together the diaper genie, organize her closet, pack my hospital bag-"

"Woah there, no wonder you look exhausted. Take a deep breath sister. I'm here to help."

"Did Hayes call you? He's annoyingly overprotective lately."

"Of course he did. He said you could use your best friend right now and was sincerely concerned that he might not survive the night if I didn't head this way right away."

Placing my hand on my stomach, I flop down into the recliner and take a deep breath. "I told you, annoyingly protective. I may or may not have threatened him with a dull butter knife."

"Ah, I remember these days. Lovingly contemplating murder at least twice a day. The good news is, you'll be able to get twice as much done in this time, and tomorrow night you and Hayes are going out for a date. All pre-planned by your baby daddy," She grins and raises her eyebrows suggestively.

I can't help the laugh that escapes, "Speaking of...things are getting more complicated than anticipated."

"I knew it. Scott owes me a new Louis!"

She squeals and jumps up and down like she's one the damn library.

"Wait, you bet on me and Hayes?"

"Duh. And I won. I said it would be pre-baby that you two finally stopped fighting each other and took the plunge. I calculated for baby hormones and forced proximity but Scott, the loser that he is, thought after the baby."

I sit up straighter, "Wait, wait, wait. You two bet on *when* not *if?* You're both on my shit list."

She doesn't look even the slightest bit ashamed. That bitch.

I say that with love. But still.

"I am so done with you."

She walks over and sits on the arm of the chair, pulling me against her side, "No you're not. This is a forever type of thing bitch, you know that. But what is more important is I need all the details. Now spill."

"It's just...he's not who I thought he was. He's *good,* Holly. He's nothing like I was determined in my head to make him. He's kind and thoughtful, and he treats me like I'm the most precious thing in the world. I love him Holly. Without a doubt."

My eyes fill with tears on their own accord and I can't stop as they spill over my cheeks.

"Oh, stop it, babe, you deserve this love and more," Holly cries as her own tears fall.

We must look a mess together, crying and hugging in the midst of a thousand onesies and dresses.

"He's proven himself, over and over, and I just don't know what I would do without him Hol. He's amazing."

"And so are you. Together, you're unstoppable. I'm so glad we tricked you two onto that boat. However unconventional it may be, look where it landed you. Even if it wasn't the plan that you made for yourself, you two are going to be amazing parents, and I know that Hayes will take care of the both of you just like you deserve."

I nod, wiping away tears.

"Now, let's dry these tears up, Mama. You and I have a lot of work to do before Hayes comes home. Not to mention, we have to find you the most perfect outfit for your date tomorrow."

"You're right. Where should we start?"

Her eyes widen as she looks around the room, "Uh, let's start in her room, this is a little overwhelming."

"Now that I can agree with."

Hours later, I hear the door slam and Hayes call, "Baby, I'm home. I have a surprise."

Holly and I look at each other, and she helps me from my spot on the couch where I've sunk in. Permanently.

"In here," I say.

He rounds the corner, a wide grin on his face as he clutches a huge pink box in his hands. Excitement shines in his eyes. He's got a pep in his step that he didn't have before he left this morning.

"I see you've recovered from my threats to do bodily harm this morning," I tease.

He walks up and sets the box down on the coffee table in front of me and drops a sweet kiss to my lips, lingering longer than he should with Holly sitting right next to me.

"God, you two get a room. I never thought I would see the day." Holly mockingly sticks her finger down her throat and gags. She gets up and tosses us a smile as she walks to the guest room that was once mine, leaving us alone.

"A present you say..." I ask.

He turns behind him and grabs the box, then hands it to me. "Well, it's for Rook, but for you too. Open it, St. James."

I smile when he calls me St. James. He still uses it affectionately even though we've crossed over the "fake" territory into something much more real. Gingerly, I remove the white bow from the package and tear at the pink paper. Once it's off, I remove the top of the white box and pull the tissue paper aside. Inside, there's a pale pink, infant sized hockey jersey with the name "Davis" on the back.

Immediately, the tears well into my eyes, and after the emotional afternoon I have had with my best friend, I lose it. Hayes' eyes widen as he drops down beside me and pulls me into his arms.

"Fuck, I'm sorry, baby I didn't mean to make you cry. I just thought it would be perfect for her. She can wear it to my games."

I sob and place my hand over my mouth. This insanely, annoyingly protective big teddy bear of a man. I am so lucky that he's mine.

"I love you," I breathe.

Placing my hands on his cheeks, the scruff brushing against my fingers, I place my lips on his and kiss him with everything I have. I want to show him, not just tell him, how much I love him and everything he does daily for both me and his daughter.

He breaks the kiss and drops his forehead to mine, "Well damn, baby, if I knew you'd love it this much, I would've brought you presents way before now."

We drink in the moment together, the true shift of things, until he speaks, "I love you, St. James. I'm glad you finally realized it."

I laugh through another sob, "Thank you. She'll love it."

"But, there's another surprise underneath." He grins.

Without pause, I move the rest of the tissue aside and look at the bottom, seeing there's a heap of clothing at the bottom. I pull it out and put the box to the side. Once I hold it up, I see that it's a gorgeous dress.

"What's this for?"

"I planned a night out in a few weeks for us, one last night with just the two of us before Rook is here."

"It's beautiful. Thank you for these gifts. Is that what you did all day, went shopping?"

His eyes twinkle, "Maybe. Not telling though. Time to feed both of my babies."

He gets up and leaves with a kiss to the cheek.

Every single day he surprises me more and more. Instead of my number one enemy, he's actually the only person I want by my side through this. My number one man.

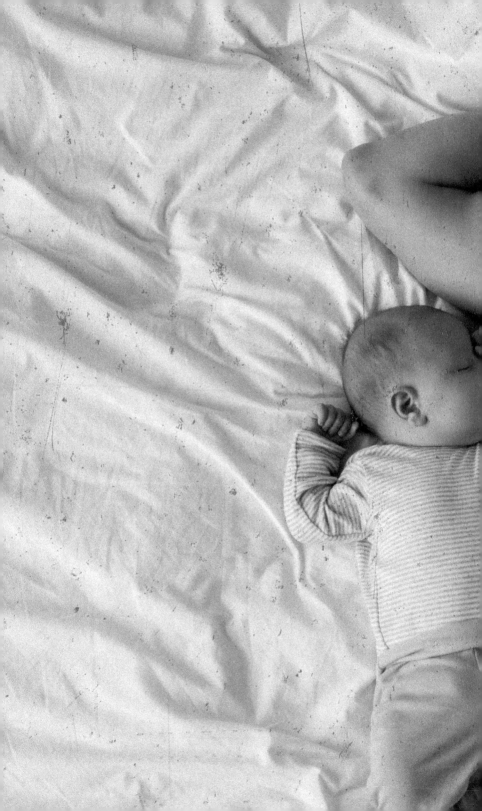

CHAPTER TWENTY

36-AND A HALF WEEKS

Hayes

Tonight is the night. I've been meticulously planning, covering every base I can possibly think of, which includes making sure our hospital bags are in the car in case of an emergency.

I'm taking Sophia to a restaurant in town that books two years in advance, which is fucking crazy because who knows what they want to eat two years in advance? But whatever. It's tastefully decorated, reeks of class, and has the most amazing lasagna in town. Sophia will love it.

"Babe, we've gotta go or we're going to miss our reservation." I call from the living room. I walk over to the mirror in the hallway and adjust my tie. I feel like it might be choking me to death, but I think that probably has something to do with my nerves.

"I'm coming, I'm coming." Her voice floats down the long hallway that leads to our room.

When I turn around, she's standing there with a small smile on her bright red lips, and goddamn, I think I've lost all train of thought.

Her long, blonde hair is curled and falling in waves down her back. The black dress I bought her fits her body like a glove. It looks incredible, like it was made just for her. She's forgone the Louboutins she loves and is in a small heel that still has me towing over her.

She's breathtaking.

"Baby...you..." I breathe.

Her cheeks flush, "I feel like a beached whale."

I close the distance between us, pulling her against me, "You are the definition of perfection, and I cannot wait to get you out of that dress. But...the heels stay." I growl.

"I might have to hobble to the bed, but if you're into it."

"Very, very into it."

She laughs as I lead her outside and lock up behind us. Once we're in the car I hold her hand the entire way to the restaurant until we pull up and the valet opens her door. When we walk in, her eyes are wide as she looks at me with excitement, and I know that it was worth the ungodly amount of money I paid to bring us here.

"Hayes, it's impossible to get in here...How?"

"Magic, babe."

The waiter leads us to a table in the back room where it's just the two of us at the Chef's table.

He'll be preparing our food tonight and bringing it out personally. Another ungodly amount of money spent to make that happen, but fuck, it was so worth it.

I pull out her chair and help her sit, taking her jacket and hanging it on the back of the chair before joining her across the table. The waiter brings our drinks and an appetizer of the best bread I've ever eaten my life, and Sophia looks at me with a smile.

"This is incredible."

"You're incredible." I tell her, "You know, I didn't just bring you here tonight because of your affection for Italian food. I knew it would make you happy, but I have an ulterior motive."

Her brow furrows in confusion.

I feel like the tie around my neck is tightening with each passing second, but somehow I manage to speak, "I love you. Our story is unconventional, and it isn't perfect by any means. But Sophia, St. James, at the end of the day, unconventional is the only love that's meant for me."

Realization crosses her face when I stand from my chair and drop down to one knee in front of her. Fat tears well in her eyes and her hand flies up to her mouth, the other I take in mine again. I can feel the tremor in her hand and I bring my lips to it.

"I never got the chance to ask you to marry me the way that you deserve. If I could do it all over, I'd make you mine from the start. Not for pretend, but forever. You are everything I will ever need or want in a woman, Sophia. The way that I love you will never fade. I want to spend every single day for the rest of forever showing you how perfect you are, worshipping you, loving you. I want to devote my life to our family. Yes, I said our, because there's nothing more in this world than I want than to put more of my babies inside you, as often as I possibly can.

She sobs and laughs at the same time as the tears pour down her face.

"Sophia St. James, will you marry me? For real this time, and for always? I need to be your husband, and not a pretend one. The real one."

The seconds tick by like hours. A drop of sweat pours down my back as I await her answer. Part of me is fucking terrified she might say no, that I might have to live apart from the only two girls I will ever need.

Then, she throws her arms around my neck and squeezes me so tight I can't even breathe while she whispers yes, over and over. I don't stop her until I pull her mouth to mine, and seal her fate.

Sophia. St James is mine, and there was never going to be pretending ever again.

"Thank fuck you said yes, or I was going to have to come up with some elaborate plan to keep you."

"Oh?" She sniffles, still laughing, until I grab her hand and slide the ring onto her finger. Confusion mars her features. "But..."

"I know. You have a ring, but it wasn't picked out by me, and it didn't feel right. This ring feels right. It's you, and it signifies my love and devotion to you."

The ring itself is a carat rose gold diamond oval, surrounded by twelve diamonds in an antique setting. It's everything I could have imagined for Sophia. When I had the jeweler make it custom,

I told him who she was, provided him photos, inspiration and he made it based upon that.

"When did you get this?"

Ah.

"I had it custom made. I think I met with him two weeks after you moved in."

Her jaw drops this time. She's in shock, and I expected nothing less.

"Yes, baby mama, fiancé, love of my life. I have known that I wanted to marry you from the few weeks you lived with me. From the very second that you sat on my couch crying over Harry Potter at midnight while you devoured Toaster Strudel...I knew. Just the mother of my child, and you're perfect for me. There was never a question. It was just a matter of when you were going to be ready to see that my feelings for you were true and that you felt the same. Took you long enough."

I wink, and drop another kiss to her lips.

"This is...surreal. It's beautiful Hayes, the absolute most perfect ring you could've ever chosen for me. This is all so beautiful and thoughtful. It means more to me than you'll ever know."

"I'm glad, baby. If you're finished, I'd really like to get you home so I can fuck you until you're screaming my name."

She looks around then cries, "Hayes!"

"I promised to always be honest with you, and I honestly can't wait to get you home so I can be buried inside of you with my ring on your finger. For real this time. You look absolutely delectable."

Her gaze darkens, and she nibbles that damn lip that drives me insane.

"I guess it's time to go then."

An hour later, we're walking through the front door, a fumble of clothes strewn around the living room. My keys land next to the table, beside my wallet. My tie is somewhere on the ottoman, and we barely make it into the bedroom before she's fumbling with the zipper of my pants.

"Baby, wait, let me help with the dress," I groan and she shakes her head, placing her lips on mine until we're both panting.

"I need you. *Now.*"

My fingers find the back of her dress in the dark, and I slowly lower the zipper, careful not to catch her. The black fabric pools at her feet and she steps out of it, breaking our kiss only to do so. She stands in front of me in matching candy apple red bra and panties, and her black heels.

"Fuck," I groan, "You're like a goddess, Sophia."

She's the epitome of my dreams. Her stomach, big and round with my baby, her skin glowing and flawless. The pink of her cheeks from my perusal of her body.

"As much as I fucking love that underwear, I want it off. Bra too. I want you naked and spread out in front of me, so I can devour you, baby."

She walks backwards until her knees hit the bed, and she sits slowly, lying back so I can remove them for her. Sex this late in pregnancy was...different, but it was not any less amazing than before. I couldn't get enough of her body.

My fucking pleasure.

I drag the lace down her hips, and reach behind her to unclasp the bra, watching as her tits spill free. They look so delectable, I can't help but dip my head and capture her nipple with my mouth. She moans when my lips close around it, threading her fingers in my hair.

"I can't wait baby, I need you," My voice is ragged with need, and she nods.

I remove the button down and slacks, then my boxers, socks, and shoes and stand before her naked, as she is. She leans forward on the bed, wrapping her hands around my cock, before she closes her mouth around my head, sucking.

Fuck, I was not expecting this. Not expecting her to put my cock in her mouth, and now I'm that much closer to losing control. The glint of her ring in the moonlight catches my eyes, and I groan.

The best moment of my entire fucking life.

If I die right now, I'll die a happy man.

I pull back, pulling myself free of her mouth, despite her protests, and help her into position on the bed, with a plush pillow beneath her. She's on her hands and knees in front of me, her ass on display, and I bend down to take a bite from her cheek, causing her to yelp.

If she wasn't pregnant, I would spank the fuck out of her, but that will have to wait until later. Bending down, I run my tongue along her pussy, from her opening to her clit, only stopping to suck her sensitive clit into my mouth. Her back arches in response. I slide my finger inside of her, and continue my assault on her clit.

"Hayes," she moans breathily, the sound barely more than a whisper. I reach below her to her tits that sway with the movement of my finger inside of her, rolling her nipple between my fingers.

I can tell from the way she begins to shake around my fingers that she's close, and I don't want her to come without being inside of her. I take the head of my cock and rub it through her slit, coating myself in her wetness before slowly pushing inside.

Fuck, it's never felt like this.

She's impossibly tight and so fucking wet for me. I slide into her until I'm seated inside of her, and her hands are fisted into the sheets as she holds on. I take my time fucking her. Drawing out my thrusts slowly, languid, with no rush until she's pushing back against me, desperate for more.

"You need more, baby?" I ask.

"Please, please, Hayes. I'm so close."

Obviously, she's listening to my desire to hear her when she needs something. I pick up the pace, slamming into her over and over, mesmerized by the way her ass shakes each time my hips meet her. She's fucking perfect.

"I'm coming," she cries, arching up onto my cock, squeezing me so tight I almost see double.

"Fuck, Sophia," I curse, grabbing onto her hips as I fall over the edge, spurting inside her. My thrusts slow as I ride out the best orgasm of my life, pulling every ounce of pleasure I can from her body. I can see she's exhausted, so I pull free from her, and help her onto her side where she sighs happily on the pillow.

"You, Mr. Davis, make me a very happy woman," she murmurs.

I laugh, then walk to the bathroom to clean up and grab a warm towel to wipe her with. After I clean up, wash my hands, and wet the towel, I walk back into the bedroom to find her standing next to the bed, a look of panic on her face.

"What's wrong?" I ask, rushing over to her. "Are you okay?"

Her eyes are wide and she's staring at the floor in disbelief before her eyes dart back up to mine, "Um...I think my water just broke."

CHAPTER TWENTY ONE

Hayes

"Breathe, or you're going to pass out," Sophia says through gritted teeth.

Shit, she's right, I expel the breath I've been holding in. Okay, think Hayes. You prepared for this. You planned for this.

Hospital bags.

Right.

"Okay, come on, St. James, we've got a baby to birth." I rub my hands down my face, trying to get my thoughts together. This was ten times easier when it was just practice and I wasn't face to face with my very pregnant fiancé and getting a front row seat to her pain.

Her eyes roll, and she winces, placing her hand on her stomach.

"Shit, that is like five minutes apart. We have to go."

"Wait, you're timing my contractions?" Her tone is surprised.

"What do you think I read that baby book twelve times for? Bags are already in the car. All I need to do is grab your pillow from the bed, and we're on our way, babe."

I grasp her hand tightly in mine as I help her out to the car and into the truck, just in time for another contraction to hit, contorting her face in pain. Her grip on my hand tightens, and I'm slightly surprised by her strength. But I've heard that women in pain are a force of nature.

"Be right back." I drop a kiss to the side of her head and run inside to grab her pillow, turn off the lights, set the alarm, and lock up. The next time we're here, we'll be carrying Rook through the front door. It's the last time I'll walk out of this door without having my girls to come home to.

The thought spreads happiness in my chest, blooming into parts of me I never knew existed.

I jog back to the truck, throw her pillow in the backseat, and get inside.

"Hayes," she says the second I slam the door shut.

"What?" I look over at her and see her knuckles turning white as she's holding onto the door handle of the truck.

"Hurry up. Please, for the love of God, *hurry* up!"

Fuck. Okay. I turn the truck on and throw it in drive, pull out onto the highway. I go eighty in a fifty-five and for the first time, Sophia doesn't complain about my driving. The closer we get to the hospital, the more intense her pain gets, and the second I screech to a stop at the emergency room entrance, she cries out in a contraction. Shockingly, my timing is impeccable.

"God, I'm so sorry, baby," I mutter, feeling absolutely helpless. I hop out of the truck and run over to her side, helping her out.

Nurses rush outside with a large wheelchair and greet us at the ramp.

"Hi, wow! It looks like it's baby time." An older nurse smiles and grabs Sophia's other hand, helping her into the wheelchair. I don't want to let her hand go for a damn second, but I have to move my truck.

"Hayes," Sophia says, "Call Holly and your family. Make sure they can get here."

"I know, baby, I will."

She nods and squeezes my hand while a smile tugs at her lips, "It's time, you over protective, annoyingly handsome daddy. Are you ready?"

"Born ready." I grin.

"Alright Dad, we need to get Mom inside and hooked up to monitors so we can watch baby's heart rate. You take care of the truck and bags and meet her inside. I'm Nurse Abby, if you need anything." The older nurse smiles and starts wheeling Sophia away.

Excitement and nerves course through me. Today is the day we've anxiously awaited for the past nine months, and it doesn't seem like it's real that it's finally here.

Today's the day I get to meet my girl.

I park the truck and grab our bags, all while juggling phone calls to notify our friends and family. Holly almost busts out my damn ear drum with her scream, and Scott quickly took the phone and said they were on the way.

Sophia and I already discussed that we would like Holly and Scott to be Rook's godparents. It seems only fitting, since they are our best friends and we're the godparents to their kids. If something did ever happen to either me or Sophia, I can't imagine anyone else but Scott and Holly raising our kids.

They are phenomenal friends and even better parents.

Fuck, this is real. I'm having a baby. We're not leaving this hospital without a baby.

I run back to the hospital, carrying all twelve bags. Okay...three bags, but they're packed so damn heavy it's like twelve, and I ask the front desk to direct me to which room she's in. I make it up to the third floor in record time, especially carrying the load that I am, and walk into chaos.

"Hayes," she screams, clutching the bed rails as Dr. Martin stands between her legs.

"Dad, it's time to have a baby. Mom is ready to push." Dr. Martin smiles.

Fuck, I think I'm going to pass out. I sway on my feet, squeezing my eyes shut, desperate for the wave of dizziness that just hit me to pass.

"You okay, Mr. Davis?" one of the nurses bustling around the room asks.

"Yes," I squeak.

I throw the bags in the nearest chair, dizziness be damned, and rush to Sophia's side, grabbing both of her hands in mine.

"It's going to be okay, baby, you're so brave, so damn strong."

Her grip on me is crushing, and she nods, taking a deep, long breath.

"Alright, Sophia, are you ready to push? On three?" Dr. Martin asks.

"It hurts," she cries, tightening her grip on my hand.

Holy fuck, we're having a baby!

The nurse hands me a damp rag, and I put it on Sophia's forehead to cool her down as the sweat pours from her. Even with her hair sticking to her forehead, mascara running down her cheeks, and her makeup completely gone, she is the most beautiful thing I've ever seen.

This moment is everything I was terrified of, and now, I am in complete awe of the woman lying before me. She's so strong.

"You are a goddess, Sophia. Hold on to me, baby, we'll get through it together and meet Rook." I smile down at her, and she softens slightly until another contraction hits her full force.

"Now, Sophia!" Dr. Martin says.

Sucking in a huge breath, she grips onto me with both hands and then expels that breath and pushes so hard the bones in my hand crack under her grip.

"That's it, baby, push." I encourage her. Wiping the damp hair from her forehead, I offer the only support that I can.

"You're doing great Sophia, just keep taking those deep breaths, and we're going to push on a contraction."

She nods.

"You're Super Woman, St. James." I tell her.

"Doesn't feel like it right now."

She gives me a small grin before resting her head on the pillow.

"I think with two more good, strong pushes, baby will be here." Dr. Martin says, "Dad, would you like to come see?"

I feel the color drain from my face. Do people do that? Watch their kids come out. My stomach churns at the thought.

"No, that's okay I think I'll just stay up here with Sophia." I mutter.

Dr. Martin laughs, "Most dads opt out, but I like to offer the option just in case it's something you are interested in. Birth is a beautiful process."

"I agree, but I would hate to end up on the floor and miss the birth of my girl."

"Hayes Davis....are you squeamish?" Sophia asks me. Another contraction hits moments later, and she's back to her death grip.

"Another strong push, Sophia, I think this will be it."

She groans, then lets out a yell that sounds so much like a fucking warrior cry going into battle, and pushes even harder this time.

Seconds later, a shrill cry fills the air, and I glance down and see Dr. Martin holding my girl, who's come out of her mother with strong, loud lungs. I wouldn't expect anything less from Rook.

People tell you about moments in their life that change them. You hear your friends, family and acquaintances talk about it,, but you never really understand what they mean until you see it for yourself.

The second I lay eyes on my daughter, my life changes right in front of my eyes. I know then that no moment that comes after will compare to seeing her take her first breath. It's like all of the things in my life led me right here, to be her dad.

Sophia sobs next to me, deep sobs that I feel in my core.

"We did it, St. James. You fucking did it. Look at her. God, look at her," I bring my lips to her head and kiss her as my own tears fall and fuck, I don't give a shit. There's nothing more beautiful than the birth of your child.

"Dad, would you like to do the honor?" Dr. Martin holds out the sterile scissors to me, and a piece of my her lifeline to Sophia to me.

The room before me sways, but I push the queasiness the fuck away, because this moment is more important. I use the clamps and cut the long cord that connects Rook to her mother, and the nurses bring her to Sophia, placing Rook on her chest.

Skin to skin, my beautiful fiancé cries and kisses her daughter, and fuck, I know in that moment, my life is complete. These girls are my world.

"What should we name her?" Sophia asks, staring at her with starry, teary eyes.

"She'll always be my Rookie, but what about Ava Maria...the same boat that brought us together?"

Sophia nods through more tears.

"Ava Maria Rook Davis, welcome to the world my girl."

Hours pass, and mostly we're allowed the luxury of bonding

together uninterrupted. Right now, Rook is swaddled in the most fucking adorable pink blanket with little hockey sticks and pucks on it, with a ridiculously large pink bow on her head. She looks like a baby doll, a real life angel. The little button of her nose, her small little lips that pucker in her sleep.

I've never in my life been happier than I am at this moment.

Sophia is finally getting some rest after breastfeeding for the first time, and I've spent the past hour watching them both sleep. To say I'm in shock and complete awe of her is an understatement. She is amazing in every sense of the world. She gave me my girl, and did it like a true champ. Ava's barely three hours old and she's already got me wrapped around her little finger, literally and figuratively. She's been clutching onto my finger with her tiny little fist for thirty minutes, and I'm scared to move an inch or take a deep breath in fear of her letting go.

Anything and everything I had imagined being a father would be like didn't even touch what it feels like to hold her in my arms. The real thing surpasses expectation tenfold. Our families will be here soon, and then our bubble of quiet as we get to know each other will be interrupted. So I'm soaking in these moments, drinking them all in while I have the chance to.

Ava sighs in her sleep and I pull out my phone to snap a few photos and send them over to Kyle, who immediately responds that he will be by later to visit. He's still hesitant about Sophia, but I think it's just his nature. He'll get over it, because I'd get rid of him before I ever thought of hurting Sophia in any way.

Life was going to be different from here on out, but it was different in the way that I'm no longer the same man as I once was. Now, my family comes first. Before hockey, appearances, magazines—any of that bullshit that I once thought I needed. My girls have filled in a spot in my life that I never even knew was missing.

My life is only now just beginning.

CHAPTER TWENTY TWO
Sophia

I'm floating on a cloud of bliss. Pure, unblemished bliss. My daughter completes my life in ways I never imagined, and seeing Hayes handle her with the utmost care?

A feeling I never expected to feel hits me square in the chest and disarms me in every possible way.

Two days ago, we were discharged from the hospital and able to come home. Ever since we walked across the threshold, Hayes has gone above and beyond to make sure I'm comfortable. Surprisingly, I'm not in as much pain as I thought I would be. Women's bodies are incredible and able to do things that are mind blowing. My body has responded well to childbirth, and now I feel like a million bucks. I can move around easily, and I have little to no pain.

What is much more challenging is breastfeeding.

Ava is latching like a pro, but I'm not creating enough milk to feed her to where she is full. So, being Hayes...he ordered at least twenty different supplements, cookies, pills, you name it, in order to help me produce more.

It's just another thoughtful gesture that proves how perfect he is.

"Hey, Soph," he calls from Ava's room. I can hear worry laced in his voice, so I walk a little faster. Although I know he's a wonderful father and handles most situations like a pro, he's still a man.

A man who freaks out over everything.

Like last night when Ava had the hiccups and he was so worried he insisted that he stay up and make sure she was breathing as she slept. And he did, until I found him passed out in the glider right next to her crib, his hand still on the wood like he could feel her move in the middle of the night.

It sent me into a bout of tears, but I'm still blaming that on the hormones, not the fact that he's the most adorably over-protective father on the planet. If she cries, he all but trips over his feet to get to her.

It's cute.

And makes me want to climb him like a tree, and I'm also blaming that on the hormones.

"Everything okay?" I ask when I walk into her room.

He's got her on the changing table, and his head is cocked to the side.

"Yeah, I was just wondering, once this falls off, will her belly button...you know, be like a normal belly button?"

"This is what you called me in here for?" I laugh, bumping his shoulder.

"I'm concerned. She's perfect, with or without this thing, but a dad's gotta know."

The concern on his face is so cute, I have to bite my lip to hold back the laugh that I am so close to letting escape. This man.

"Hayes, she's fine and will have a perfectly normal belly button."

He visibly relaxes, "Phew. Was worried there for a second, Rook, but don't worry, Daddy will love you, always. Even if you have a weird belly button." He talks to her, grinning as he rubs his thumb over sweet cheeks.

That's it.

Ovaries. Exploding.

I sigh, placing my head on his arm and watching the two of them together.

"Alright, quit hogging the baby, mister. Let me get her ready for bed, and you and I are in need of some QT time."

I'm teasing, but the way that his eyes darken shows me that he is missing our intimacy as much as I am. Too bad. Per doctor's orders, I'm out of commission for at least another four weeks.

"Okay, I'm just going to lay across the bed for five minutes. In case she cries."

I laugh, "Hayes. I've got this. Go rest."

Finally, he grudgingly transfers her into my arms and drops a chaste, quick kiss to my lips before wandering out of her room down the hall into our room. I go through our nighttime routine, giving her a bath with lavender wash and lotion, changing her into a fresh pair of pajamas, cuddling her to my chest all the while and taking in every single moment.

I feel like being a mother is what I've always been meant to be.

After a few minutes of rocking her and singing her the same lullabies my mother sang me as a child, she drifts off to sleep. I make sure to swaddle her tight and place her in her crib. Monitor in hand, I make my way down the hall and find Hayes passed out face first in the bed.

I poke him gently with my foot to make sure he's still breathing, and sure enough he snores so loudly that I'm sure he's woken up Ava.

"You crazy man." I sigh, pulling his shoes off and putting them to the side of the bed. "So exhausted you pass out with shoes on."

He grumbles in his sleep but still remains as dead asleep as a log.

I take the moments of silence and some of my first moments alone as a mother, and take a long, hot bath. My muscles and body are still somewhat sore from birth and recovery. I spend so long in the bath, staring at Ava on the monitor, that I've turned pruny. She's soundly sleeping, much like her daddy in the other room. I can hear his deep snores through the bathroom door. I want to try and get a few hours of sleep before Ava wakes up to feed, so I get out, even though the warm water is still like heaven to my muscles, and dry off. I throw on an old t-shirt of Hayes' to get into bed.

"Hayes, wake up." I say softly in his ear.

His eyes snap open and he jumps up, completely disoriented.

"I'm coming, Ava." His voice is rough and full of sleep.

I giggle, "Woah, calm down, Ava's fine big guy."

How a six-foot-four, manmade of pure lethal muscle can be so wrapped around this little girl's finger blows my mind. When it comes to her, he's completely soft.

He drags his hand down his face, trying to wake up, "I'm sorry, baby, I must've passed out. Did you get her to sleep?"

I nod, "Yep, all tucked in and asleep." I show him the monitor that's focused on her bed, showing him her sleeping soundly.

"Maybe I should go check on her? Just to make sure everything is okay." He starts to get up from the bed, but I push him back down by his shoulders and straddle his lap.

"No, let her sleep. Opening the door might wake her. She'll let us know when she needs to eat or be changed." I put my finger under his chin and drag his eyes from the monitor to mine, "You are the best daddy, Hayes. It makes me so happy to see how attentive and careful you are with her. But you have to take care of yourself too. That means sleeping, in your bed, for more than an hour at a time before you're up and checking on her, or sleeping next to her bed. She is okay."

"I'm just worried that something will happen if I'm not there."

"I know, and it's a legitimate fear, but we have to know that, as her parents, we're doing the best that we can, and we're making sure she is protected and safe."

He thinks about what I'm saying before he speaks. His face relaxing, "You're right. Maybe I'll go to the gym or something. Just to get out of the house, hang with the guys."

"Go, babe, you deserve it. She and I will have a girl's day and relax here at the house. Mani's and crappy reality television. Or hey, even better, I'll put on a horror movie and get her started early."

He gives me a look that says he doesn't find me at all amusing and I throw my head back and laugh, "See. Overprotective. We'll be fine. Tomorrow, I'm kicking you out for the whole day. It's done."

"Fine, but I'm going to FaceTime you and see both of your faces because I love you both so fucking much."

"I know, and we love you, babe. Let's get some sleep?"

He nods, "I can't wait until Dr. Martin clears you and I can have my way with you, because, St. James, being a mother, makes you that much hotter. I think we should have more...starting now."

"Okay, Casanova. Sleep, then we'll talk about more baby making, 'Kay?"

A wide grin tugs at the corner of his lips, "Fine."

CHAPTER TWENTY THREE

Hayes

'm turning into a complete pussy. I might as well walk right up to Sophia St. James and hand her my man card, wrapped in a frilly pink bow.

And I don't even care. *Not in the least.*

Excitement has replaced my nerves, with my fears taking a back burner. Sure, I don't know what the fuck I'm doing, but with Sophia by my side, I have no doubt that we're going to kick this parenting thing's ass.

Not to mention, my daughter has me so far wrapped around her finger, there's no chance I'm resurfacing anytime soon. She's so perfect and so beautiful that it takes my breath away.

When Sophia told me she was kicking me out for the day, last week, I felt panic, pure fucking panic at the thought of leaving either of them for even a short amount of time. Part of me thought, "Not ready! Not even close." But she was right—I needed fresh air and a moment to breathe. Even if I was going to obsess over them the entire time.

So, I got out. Went to the gym, met the guys from the team for lunch. They showered Ava with ridiculous gifts, and then I was ready to come home. That was long enough away from them.

That was my first outing, and I've only left them here twice since in the four weeks that we've been home together.

Generally, I go to the rink and skate with the guys, but as soon as I'm gone, I want to be home with my girls. I'm not looking forward to the season starting. I don't know how I'll handle being away from them for any extended period of time. I'm not going to, that's how. I'll figure it out, and I'll make it work.

After a long, grueling workout, I'm pulling up at the house, finally.

God, I can't wait to kiss Soph and hold my girls.

"Baby, I'm home," I call softly, throwing my keys into the basket by the front door and toeing off my Nikes.

Silence greets me, so I figure they must be taking a nap. Not that I blame her— uninterrupted sleep is few and far between now, and she should be taking every second she can and sneaking in a nap.

Plus, that means I get more time with Ava and can hog her all to myself. I grin.

I walk into the kitchen in search of something to eat, and Sophia's sitting at the kitchen table with a look I don't think I'll ever forget. Hurt, anger. Silent tears rest on her cheeks and she doesn't speak when our eyes connect across the room.

Holy shit, what happened?

"Sophia, is it Ave? Are you okay? Where is she?" I rush over to her and she puts up her hand to stop me.

What the fuck is going on? I ask myself.

She's cold and aloof, and now she doesn't want me near her?

"Ava is fine. I'm fine." Her voice is broken, and fuck, something inside of me cracks.

I don't understand, everything was fine when I left for the gym this morning.

"What happened? Tell me what's going on; you're scaring the fuck out of me."

Her eyes drop down to the object on the table, and only then do I notice that there's something in the middle of the kitchen table.

Red and lacy...it looks like lingerie. Nothing like something she would wear.

"Your puck bunny dropped this off this morning after a short visit."

"The fuck? Why the fuck was someone at my house uninvited?" I ask, trying to close the distance between us, but she looks like she might actually murder me if I step another inch towards her. I'm lost. I have no idea what the fuck is going on.

"Becca? Beth? Sorry, I couldn't really focus on her name when she busted past me into the house."

"What?" Rage fills my veins at the thought of someone coming into my house, someone fucking touching Sophia. Someone threatening my daughter's safety? Hell no.

Calm down, Davis.

"Tell me what happened, Sophia."

Her eyes narrow before she speaks, "The other night when you said you were at the rink, putting extra hours in, were you really with her?"

"What!? Fuck no, I was on the ice skating, running drills. Why would I ever be with another woman who wasn't you or Ava?"

She shrugs then gestures to the underwear on my table. The red stark against the cream-colored table.

It dawns on me after a moment that she's talking about the girl from before we were together, the same one Kyle's been telling me has been contacting him, saying it's urgent she speaks with me. She's been hanging on like a bad fucking dream. Kyle's threatened her with a restraining order, but it just seems to make her want me more. The fact that I'm unobtainable and want her to leave me the fuck alone, and the fact that I didn't want to bother Sophia with this drama during her birth or our time with Ava afterward.

Apparently, Ava's birth in the tabloids is making her seek me out again. Desperate for attention.

"She said she was dropping by to see you after your night together the other night. Wanted to leave this," she glances at the underwear, "for you. Said to tell you that she misses you and can't wait to see you."

"What the fuck. Sophia, list-"

She cuts me off by standing from the chair abruptly, the legs scraping against the hardwood. "Do not, Hayes. I don't want to hear it. You know, after the past couple of weeks, I really thought that this was going to work. I really thought that somehow in this crazy situation that we were going to be alright. You had me completely fooled. Utterly. The ring, the doting father, all of it. Was it all a lie?"

Tears stream down her cheeks, and a part of me dies. I'm causing those tears, but if she'd just listen then I could explain.

My jaw tightens, my teeth beginning to ache from how tight I'm holding it. Fuck. This is the worst shit that could happen to us, now.

"I thought you were making a real effort. To be different, to be better. For our child. You truly had me fooled. All you've done is show me that you'll never change. You'll always be the playboy. This child and I don't fit your lifestyle, and we never will."

"Sophia, wait," I step towards her, and she takes a step backwards, "the girl is obsessed with me. I swear to you, I was at the rink, not with some girl that means absolutely nothing to me. You think I'd risk this? My family?" The word feels weird coming from my lips, but that's what we are, aren't we? Even as unconventional and ass backwards as it is, these girls are my family. "I would never disrespect you or make a fool of you. I love you. I love Ava, I would do anything for you. I'd never be with another woman."

She crosses her arms over her chest while another tear falls from her eyes, another piercing arrow to my heart. "I just know what she said, Hayes. Isn't this exactly who you've always been? Hayes the playboy. She knew exactly where you were just now.

How did she know that?"

"Fuck, I don't know Sophia. I haven't even seen her since months before we even got together," I run my fingers through my hair, frustrated.

"You never even asked me why it was that I hated you so badly. Don't you remember how badly you hurt me when we were kids?"

What is she talking about?

She laughs haughtily, "Judging by the look on your face, you have no clue. You broke my heart, Hayes, and it never even crossed your radar. Remember ninth grade, when you and your friends decided to place that bet? The one that meant you'd take me to prom, and no one else thought I'd agree to it. St. James the nerd. Right?"

I try and think back to those days. Fuck, I was just a fucked-up kid.

"You asked me to prom, and I was so excited. I'd had the biggest thing for you for years, and finally, I thought, finally you'd noticed me. I was so much chunkier then, teased relentlessly for it. And finally, you had taken notice of me and the childish crush I had for you. I bought the perfect dress, spent hours on my makeup and hair, still pinching myself that Hayes Davis, the Hayes Davis, was taking a freshman, me, to prom." She pauses, shaking her head, "Then seven came, and it went. Then eight, then nine, and you never showed up."

What is she even talking about? Hell, I barely remember high school, period. I skated by in classes by the skin of my teeth.

Oh, fuck. When I was sick. I thought I told her I was out of my mind on every cough medicine in the world? Prescription strength stuff. I was sick as shit.

"I got the flu, Sophia, I hardly even remember prom night. I'm so fucking sorry that I hurt yo-"

She stops me, "That was the night I realized that no matter how much of a pedestal they put you on, you'd always be the same person who stood me up that night. Who took my already broken self-confidence, and made a fool of me. It might seem silly to you, to hold on to something like that, but I never forgot. Having to be around you most of my adult life because of Scott and Holly was just the icing on the cake. I trusted you. I stopped letting the past live in the future, and I trusted you. And all you did was prove me right in every way. That you're still that boy who has no regard for anyone that he hurts."

"Sophia, wait, stop le—"

"No. I won't let you hurt me or Ava because you can't commit to anything, or anyone."

She slides the ring free from her finger, the same one that I just gave to her months ago, confessed my love. Every single word I meant, and I still do in this moment, even though she's looking at me with so much hate in her eyes that it sends me back a few staggering steps.

"I can't believe that I fell for it. I fell for you and all of the lies that you spewed, and I fell right into the trap. Now, we're not kids in high school anymore, Hayes. Your actions have consequences.

We're not two kids who have nothing to lose. We have a daughter, and she will come first, always. My broken heart will take a back seat to her, always.".

"We're leaving and staying with Holly for a while. I need out of this house. I need to be anywhere that you aren't right now. Burn the kitchen table, I'm scared you might get an STD from touching that." She brushes past me, her sweet scent invading my heart in ways I never planned, and leaves me standing there with no clue what the hell just happened, or any idea how to fix it.

The next week is the worst form of torture. Sophia hasn't spoken one word to me, which is very fucking hard when all I can do is think about her and Ava and the fucking mess I'm in. She makes sure to send me photos of Ava and allows me to Facetime her whenever I want, but it's just not the same. I miss my girls. I miss my woman, and I'm at a total fucking loss.

I want them home.

I fucking miss her. I miss her laugh and the way that her nose crinkles when a smell hits her that doesn't agree with her stomach. I miss watching her with Ava, cuddling her to her chest as she breastfeeds her, in complete awe of her strength.

I know now that even though I wasn't really with another female, Sophia's hurt runs deep. It's the core reason she didn't trust me in the first place, and now I have to do whatever it takes to make it better. How could I not remember prom? Why didn't I push harder to understand the bitterness between us all these years?

Truth be told, I'd thought it was our fucked-up way of flirting. I didn't see how deep her betrayal ran—how much I'd truly hurt her. And I'll spend forever making up for that.

The first thing I do is call Kyle and let him know what happened. I'm going to meet him downtown at the station in the next two hours to file an official restraining order and report for stalking. She took it too fucking far. She threatened my child's safety. Who the fuck busts into the house of someone they had a one-night stand with?

A crazy person, that's who. Which is why I'm following through with the report and restraining order, because she doesn't get to think that's okay.

It's not. Next, I call the security company and have them come out to install a new state of the art system with every upgrade and customization they offer. When I get my girls home—and I will be getting them home—I want Sophia to feel completely safe and not worry that this will ever happen again.

Even though her issue is with me, not security, I need to know that they will be safe.

Now, I'm getting my girls, and I know exactly what I need to do.

I dial the one person who will be on my side, even if her loyalty lies with Sophia.

"Holly…"

CHAPTER TWENTY FOUR

Sophia

I hate him.

No, that's a lie. The same one I've been telling myself over and over since we arrived at Holly and Scott's. I collapsed, sobbing, into my best friend's arms and prayed that this would be over soon. That the hurt would lessen and I could be the pillar of strength that Ava would need going forward.

But I hurt. I hurt so bad I can feel the pain in my bones. Aching. Reminding me of what I've lost.

I can't eat. I can't sleep. I can't stop feeling the bitter sting of betrayal when I think of Hayes. How could he do this? How could he rip our family apart...for a puck bunny?

He chose his old life and left me and Ava to find our way without him.

It hurts.

"Soph, do you want a sandwich?" Holly asks from the kitchen.

"No, thank you." I mutter.

Ava is staring up at me with wide, curious eyes, and I thank

God for her. I can't imagine how much it would hurt if I didn't have my daughter by my side because, even through all of this, she brings me so much happiness. She's the only reason I've even been able to muster a smile in the past week.

Five whole days since I left him. Five days since I packed all of our stuff and came to stay with Holly and Scott. Five days since I've touched him or inhaled his scent.

The thought of those things brings another fresh batch of tears to my eyes.

I switch between anger and hurt, sometimes with the anger weighing out over the hurt. I'm angry at him for doing this to not only me, but to Ava. She deserves better, and I'm sad that he proved me right. It's not what I wanted.

"Soph, how about we take the kids to the park this evening? Get out of the house, stretch our legs, and get some fresh air. I think we could all use it."

Holly walks back into the living room and smiles at me. She pities me, and I hate that feeling worst of all.

"Sounds good." I give her a watery, fake smile that she sees right through.

"Maybe you should just talk to him, Soph. Hear him out—see what he has to say. It might surprise you."

I whip around to look at her, "You've talked to him?"

The traitor.

She shrugs, "No, but Scott has. He's hurting too, Soph. I've never seen Hayes like this."

"It doesn't mean he isn't guilty."

"I'm just saying. What if all of this is just a big misunderstanding?"

"I doubt it. I'm going to put Ava down for a nap; I'll be ready to go to the park tonight."

I get up and leave Holly in the living room. I'm hurt, and I don't want to hear sensibility from her. I want her to tell me he's an asshole and that she'll slash his tires with me if I want to, which I don't—but if I did. She's always been my ride or die, but right now it feels like she isn't picking a side.

And it causes me to doubt.

Should I have given him more of a chance to explain? What was there to explain about this? The evidence is there, cut and dry.

Right?

I sigh, rocking Ava to me, waiting for her curious, bright eyes to drift to sleep so I can let the tears I've been holding back fall.

None of this feels right. It doesn't feel right to have the man I'm hopefully in love with break my heart into a billion pieces. To have him betray me by doing the one thing I needed him to never do.

Make me lose my trust.

"Why did Scott want to drive the kids again?" I ask Holly. I'm starting to feel the slightest bit on edge, because it doesn't seem like we're headed in the direction of the park. "Holly, where are we going?"

253

She looks at me with a guilty expression, "Not to the park."

My eyes widen, "I knew it!" I sigh, "I knew you were up to something when you asked about the park. Tell me where we're going right now before I punch you in the vagina. Don't tempt me; I am feeling extra violent today."

"This is me, as your lifelong best friend, intervening and making sure you pull your head out of your ass and don't lose the man who loves you and your daughter with everything he has."

"So you are on his side? That's what you're saying?" I cross my arms over my chest, pulling my gaze from her.

"No, that is not what I'm saying. What I'm saying is that I'm not picking sides. I love you Soph, with all of my heart. Enough to mess with your life like it's my right if it means that I'll make you happy in the end. Just hear him out. Hear what he has to say. That's all I'm asking as your best friend: just hear him out."

I clench my jaw and continue looking out the window. It's a little too late to be able to say no, right?

We drive further and further out of town, closer to the bay side and soon, the same marina that this whole mess started at comes into view.

Well, if this isn't full circle. Holly interfering, again. Trapping us on the same boat, again.

"Really?" I ask.

She shrugs, "I'm just dropping you two off. This is all him." She puts the car into park and gets out, helping me with Ava's car seat and bag.

"Over there." She points to the yacht that we were supposed to have our photoshoot on.

What in the world is going on?

"I'm not going." I say, even though I feel childish throwing a fit over it. I'm hurt, and the last thing I want to do is come face to face with him.

"You're going. Trust me, Soph, okay?" Holly says softly before she pulls me in for a tight hug. I hug her back after a few seconds, then she releases me and nods towards the boat. "Go get your man."

Right.

My stomach is in knots. I glance down at my sleeping daughter and see a small smile on her face, and it gives me the courage to get this over with.

If anything, maybe it will offer some closure.

I find the boat that's lit up with a string of lights, sparkling and bright; they call out to me like a beacon, the name "Ava Marie" scrawled across the side, and I know I'm in the right place. The nerves in my stomach jumble around, making me nauseous about coming face to face with Hayes for the first time since I left.

And just like that, he appears from the side of the boat, looking so handsome, so perfect that it causes my stomach to turn. Even with how angry and betrayed I feel, I can't help my body's reaction to him.

He's wearing a tux, complete with a bow tie, and his hair is gelled and not falling into his face like usual. He looks breathtaking, and oh does he steal the breath right from my lungs.

The closer I get, the heavier each step toward him feels. Finally, I make it to the opening that beckons me on, asking for me to step back onto the boat that brought us together in the first place, but my hurt supersedes the feelings from the last time I was here.

"Hi," he whispers, giving me a sad grin. It's the least favorite one I've ever seen upon his lips, but it's beautiful nonetheless.

Hayes Davis could be the devil himself, with the smile of an angel, and still blind everyone in the room with how handsome he is.

"Hi," I say back.

"Thank you for coming."

"Didn't have much of a choice."

He nods, "Holly."

"Yeah."

He steps forward to see Ava, and I instinctively flinch when his tuxedoed arm brushes mine.

"Sorry," he says, but the hurt is written on his face.

"Don't be. She's smiling now," I say, nodding towards Ava.

"Hey, Daddy's sweet girl," he coos as he unbuckles her from her seat and pulls her out, clutching her tightly against his chest.

Then I almost regret leaving in the first place, no matter how hurt I am. Almost. It's not as if I'm taking Ava from him. I would never do that. I just have to put space between the two of us, and her being attached to my boob twenty-four seven means she's coming with me.

"Daddy has missed you so much, Rook. So much."

My heart is ready to explode at the exchange, and I can't help the tears that well in my eyes. This just feels all wrong. My family completely ripped in half by his horrible decisions.

I wish that we could rewind time—erase it all and go back to the love that surrounded us daily when we were together.

"Sophia?" he asks, pulling me from my thoughts.

The next thing I know, he's carrying Ava and her car seat onto the boat with me following closely behind. The gentle sway and rock of the waves is calming, and I pause for a second, taking a deep breath and trying to gain my composure.

I know that what happens next will change us, and part of me isn't ready for it.

Hayes sets Ava back in her carrier, then places her soft pink blanket on top of her, tucking her in, all the while telling her how much he loves her.

"Sophia, I know you are angry at me. And the last place you want to be is here, but please hear me out and listen to what I have to say."

I cross my arms over my chest and take a seat on the bench opposite of him.

"Fine."

He nods, then pulls a paper from the inside pocket of his jacket. I wish I could run my finger along the furrowed part of his brow that's bunched in frustration. Angry as I am, I can't help my pull to him.

"You're probably wondering why here?"

I nod, but say nothing.

"I bought it."

My jaw hangs open in shock, "Wait, you what? Hayes...this yacht has to cost millions of dollars." My mind reels at the price tag, and yes, he's a wealthy professional hockey player, but a yacht?

"Doesn't matter. This yacht will forever be a place of happiness for me. It's where I fell for you for the first time, and didn't even know it yet. Watching you dance around, drunk off your ass from cheap tequila, to that god awful nineties music that made my fucking ears bleed. God, I was crazy for you. I should've realized it then."

I bite my lip to hold back a smile.

"And then, the Ava is where we made Rook. It's her namesake, and it's important to me. I want it to be a part of our lives. I know you're angry, St. James, and if I was you, blindsided by something like that, I would be too. But I want you to know I would never cheat on you. I would never betray you. and I would never do anything that would harm our family."

He walks closer and holds out the piece of paper he took out of his jacket. My hand shakes as I take it and run my eyes down it as best I can with only the dim lights from the yacht. What I think I'm looking at is a police report. I see...stalking and a restraining order?

"What is this?"

"That's the police report that I filed, as well as the restraining order that was filed against her. If she comes within a thousand feet of any of us, including you, she's going to jail. I didn't sleep with her, Soph. Fuck, I didn't even think of that woman until you brought it up to me. All I've seen is you; that's why I was so shocked when the name dawned on me. The fact that she showed up to my home, which she had never been to by the way, and pushed her way inside? Fuck no. Our home is a place where we're supposed to feel safe, and for someone so crazy to pull some shit like that…I wasn't playing around." He sits next to me on the bench and takes my hands, looking me in the eyes. I can see his sincerity, and I feel the walls of my heart beginning to crack, "I upgraded the security system to a fucking fortress. If anyone comes within a hundred feet of the house and does anything including sneeze, the police department will be there in three minutes or less. Not that I think she'll be a problem anymore. With her name plastered on social media for stalking me—thanks to Kyle and the story he leaked— she's probably on her way out of the country."

"If you want to move out of the house and find another one, I'll sell it. We can pick a house out together. Fix it up, build it—I truly don't give a shit as long as I have my girls home."

I open my mouth to speak, but he stops me, "Not yet, baby. Listen. Then I realized that, while this psycho is the reason this happened, there was more. There are things that we never worked through, never talked about, lurking beneath the surface, and it's truly what made you doubt me. The way I treated you in the past… the person that I used to be. I'm not at all proud of that, and I wish that I could take it back, but I can't. All I can do is prove to you from this day forward that you and Ava are my life, my entire fucking life, and I will never ever do anything to jeopardize what we have."

He stands, bringing me with him, his hands laced with mine, still gentle and hesitant.

"I believe you, Hayes."

"You do?" His eyes widen.

"I do. While it was a complete shock to come face to face with someone from your past throwing out these crazy scenarios, part of me was waiting for the other shoe to drop. I shouldn't have thrown accusations at you. I should've given you a chance to explain, but I was so blinded by the familiar betrayal that I just had to get out and get away. It was too much. I'm sorry too, I'm sorry I let my own insecurities win."

"I understand. I gave you space because I didn't want to push you so far that I'd never get you back. My life is nothing without the two of you, Soph. You're it for me. We never got to dance at prom…so I want to dance with you now—dance with you and Ava forever."

He puts his hand in his pocket and pulls out my ring that I foolishly gave back to him out of hurt and anger. Regret flashes in my heart seeing the look on his face.

"This is yours, and I hope that with it, we can start fresh—that we can let go of the past and not let those mistakes and hurtful things define our future. I love you, Sophia, and I want to be your husband. I want to be the man that heals your heart, no matter who breaks it."

The tears finally break free, and I hold my shaking hand out for him to slide the ring back on my hand. Once it's secure, I launch myself into his arm and kiss him. He takes my mouth roughly, with all of the frustration that he's likely been holding in since our fight.

Breaking free, he says, "Please don't ever fucking leave me again. I can't handle it, St. James."

I nod and seal my lips over his again, whispering my promises against his lips until his tongue teases the seam of my lips, slipping inside my mouth and dancing to the familiar dance that we once did right here on this boat.

"I'm yours, forever. Unless you threaten to hide my Toaster Strudel again, then...I'm not responsible."

He laughs and pulls me closer against him until Ava's cry breaks us apart.

Our life isn't going to always be easy, and neither will our marriage. Love isn't easy. Love is a journey. It must be fought for, sacrificed for, and handled with care. Sometimes you have to compromise on the things you swore you never would. Sometimes you have to change into the person you said you'd never become. And sometimes you fall for your number one enemy, who turns out to be the very best thing that ever happened to you.

Hayes Davis is the country's number one hockey player and America's sweetheart, but he's also my best friend, my real husband to be, and the best daddy on the planet.

Suck it, puck bunnies. He's mine.

EPILOGUE

Hayes

EIGHT MONTHS LATER

BEEP BEEEEEEEP BEEEEEEP.

The shrill sound of the smoke alarm is sounding as thick, dark smoke billows out from inside the oven—sure sign that the dinner I've been working on for the past two hours is ruined.

"Fuck," I curse, grabbing the oven mitts from the island and using them to waft away the thick smoke as I make my way over to the smoking oven. I'm racking my brain trying to figure out where I went wrong. Did she say an hour or thirty minutes?

Does it really matter now? Damnit, what in the hell am I doing? The closest I've come to cooking is ramen noodles in the microwave or a TV dinner, if I'm feeling fancy. This is Sophia's area of expertise, but I wanted to do something nice for her since she's been working so hard in class.

I look over at Ava, who's covered in pureed fruit, sucking on her fist in her high chair.

My beauty is cute as ever, even covered head to toe in sweet potatoes.

"My sweet potato, did you actually get any of that in your mouth?" I ask, scratching my head, grinning when she gives me a belly laugh.

"Da Da, Da, Da, Da," she squeals.

The two of us are a complete mess, yet somehow perfect together.

Sophia decided when Rook turned four months old that she wanted to go back to school to become a kindergarten teacher, and of course I told her that I support any and every dream that she will ever have. Which means, when I'm not at the rink, it's just me and Rook.

I'm like the six-foot-four version of Mrs. Doubtfire, except I'm a helluva lot more handsome, if you ask me.

"Call me Mr. Mom, Rook." I grin when she talks back to me in baby gibberish that I won't even begin to attempt to decipher. I'm just happy to see her toothless grin.

The front door opens and slams just as I've turned the oven off and tossed the blackened, charred lasagna into the sink.

"Hayes?"

Sophia's standing by the island, squinting at me through the smoke.

"St. James. Perfect timing," I grunt.

She laughs before walking closer, and I sigh, then pull her in for a kiss that leaves us both breathless. When she pulls back, she looks at me, "Did you...cook?" Her nose squints in distaste.

"Don't sound so surprised. You see how it turned out."

"Umm...what was it?" She giggles, gesturing to the charred mess in the sink that is still smoking.

"Lasagna."

"Ah, the Gordon Ramsey go-to."

She sees right past my bullshit, "That obvious?"

"No, but Holly called me after you called her and said I might want to get home before you burned our house down."

"Well, at least I tried. I wanted to take a load off of you since you have so much to study for. If it counts, Rook helped me make the sauce."

"Did she?"

She walks over to Ava and picks her up from the high chair, laughing when she sees just how much sweet potato she's covered in.

"Straight to the bath for you, missy. Thank you for trying, handsome." She gives me a sweet kiss before brushing past me to Ava's bathroom for a much-needed bath.

"Take out it is Mademoiselle. Chinese? Greek? Italian? Take your pick." I call down the hallway and pull out the stacks of takeout menus I have in the drawer next to the oven—the most logical place for a man who hasn't cooked anything that wasn't processed in his entire life.

"Mmm, Fun Shu chicken is calling my name. I think I've been craving it," I hear her voice float down the hallway.

Never fails. Sophia is a Chinese girl through and through. I should've known before I asked. One of these days, she was going to surprise me though.

After I call in the food, I quickly pick up the living room, genuinely wondering how an eight-month-old is able to create this much mess. There are tiny toys scattered on every surface of the living room...and under the couch, and behind the couch, and on top of the entertainment center...

I laugh when I pick the block up and put it back in her toy box.

"Mmm, do you know how hot it is to see you pick up toys? Honestly, it's so damn hot." Sophia walks into the living room and flops onto the couch. Her blonde hair is piled high on her head, and she's got dark bags under her eyes. She looks exhausted, and I want more than anything to take some of it away. If that means picking up toys and taking care of Rook while she studies... consider it done.

"There's more where that came from, St. James," I tease, putting the boxes back away in Ava's play center. "Today we went to the rink, and the guys spent an hour passing her around, blowing raspberries and doting on her like a bunch of saps. I got lots of pictures for blackmail."

She laughs and gestures me over to her.

"Thank you. Seriously, Hayes, for picking up my slack and being the best partner and daddy around. It means the world to me to have your support."

I bring her hand to my lips and kiss her ring on her left finger,

"For better or worse, baby. I promised to stand by your side."

"I cherish these moments. The moments of peace and quiet, where I can just breathe."

Christmas is right around the corner, and I plan to surprise her with a getaway to the mountains for her and Ava since she'll be on break for school, but it feels so far away, even though it's just over a month away. With school and wedding planning, she's beyond exhausted. She deserves a week in the mountain to catch up on sleep and feel rejuvenated.

I take her feet in my hands and rub circles on the bottoms, telling my dick to chill when she starts to moan in pleasure.

Not that he ever listens but...

"Hey, I forgot to ask, I have a friend who's just been hired as the head coach in Chicago, and he's looking for a nanny. You wouldn't happen to know of anyone? You know, in that giant-ass group text all of you have?"

She laughs, "Just because I've made friends with all of the hockey wives doesn't mean I keep up with their nannies, Hayes. But I'll ask Jessica. I think her husband plays for Chicago now."

"You're the best," I grin and drop my lips to hers. "He's having hard time. His wife passed away a few years ago, and he can't pass this job up, so he needs someone for his daughter. I just think about Rook and what would happen in a situation like that."

"You have the biggest heart. You're much more of a giant teddy bear than I imagined."

"C'mon on, St. James, can you not compare me to a damn

teddy bear? My masculinity can't handle it." I wince.

"How about we go work on making you feel better then. I've been reading this new book...." Her eyebrows raise, and she gives me a smile that tells me everything I need to know.

"I think there's going to be a lot of kissing and making me feel better involved in this."

"Oh, you have no idea."

"I love you, Sophia St. James."

"And I love you. Is it the right time to mention that I want a brother for Rook? We had a long talk last week. You know...me and Ava."

I throw my head back and laugh, "Oh is that so?"

She nods and gives me a nonchalant shrug, "We've got lots of time to practice."

And that's exactly what we did.

Practice.

Thank you SO much for reading The Enemy Trap! I hope you loved these two as much as I did. And guess what… they came a cameo in my next release, The Newspaper Nanny!

Hayes's friend Liam is in desperate need of a new nanny after he takes the job as Chicago's head coach.

What happens when the grumpiest coach in the NHL needs a new nanny?

The playoff of a lifetime.

Join my reader group and be the first to know! Give Me Moore

Maren's first book was more of a success than I could've ever hoped for! Thank you so much.

When I decided to create my Maren pen name, I was nervous. I wasn't sure if there was a market for it, I wasn't sure if any of my other readers would come over to the light side with me. I wasn't sure if I would be able to write Romcom the way that I do my dark stuff.

But, I decided to do it anyway.

And I am so glad that I didn't let fear stop me.

As always, I want to thank my team for going above and beyond. I truly believe that without them, I wouldn't be able to function.

Jac, you are a ray of light in my life, and quite honestly the best PA on the planet, even if I am a bit bias. You run my life seamlessly, and make everything so easy. Thank you for all of your hard work, and dedication to making my books what they are. I love you!

Katie, my plot fairy. You know how dire you are to my process. I can't live without you. Love you!

Haley, my beta and the sweetest friend on the planet. I appreciate you so very much. Thank you for helping me make this book what it is!

Alexandria, my spicy little Canadian. I just adore you. Your feedback is so vital to making sure my books are what they are and I can't imagine my team without you on it. ILY!

Jos, my hype girl, so much love to you babe! For inspiring me for a future book you have no idea about yet ;)

Elijah, my best babe, for inspiring me ENDLESSLY with your graphics, even when I tell you literally nothing about an idea, and you help me bring it to life. You are my sounding board, and I love you!

Karen & Mia, my girls forever. I'm not sure what I would do without either of you. I love you both so much.

Rach, Britt, Shawna, Jes, Kristina - I found my tribe with you, and I'm keeping you.

To my street team, and to my Facebook group Give Me Moore. Thank you for all of the hard work that you do. You share, repost, comment and hype my books and it is so very much appreciated.

And as always, thank you to the readers who pick this up and take a chance on me. Whether you loved or hated it, the fact that you took the chance means everything. Without you, our world wouldn't turn.

Maren Moore is the alter ego of R. Holmes, author of dark, angsty and forbidden romance. Desperate to let the lighter, fluffier side reign free, she created Maren.

You can always expect alphas and HEA's that are dripping of sweetness from her.

CPSIA information can be obtained
at www.ICGtesting.com
Printed in the USA
BVHW081104271221
624882BV00006B/195

9 781087 996929